Helle Helle

THIS SHOULD BE WRITTEN
IN THE PRESENT TENSE

Translated from the Danish by
Martin Aitken

Harvill Secker

LONDON

Published by Harvill Secker 2014

2 4 6 8 10 9 7 5 3 1

Published in agreement with the Gyldendal Group Agency

First published with the title *Dette burde skrives i nutid* in 2011
by Samleren, Copenhagen

First published in Great Britain in 2014 by
HARVILL SECKER
Random House
20 Vauxhall Bridge Road
London SW1V 2SA

www.vintage-books.co.uk

Addresses for companies within The Random House Group Limited
can be found at: www.randomhouse.co.uk/offices.htm

The Random House Group Limited Reg. No. 954009

A CIP catalogue record for this book is available from the British Library

ISBN 9781846558054 (hardback)
ISBN 9781448182930 (ebook)

This publication was assisted by a grant from the Danish Arts Foundation

**STATENS KUNSTFOND
THE DANISH ARTS FOUNDATION**

The Random House Group Limited supports the Forest Stewardship
Council® (FSC®), the leading international forest-certification organisation.
Our books carrying the FSC label are printed on FSC®-certified paper.
FSC is the only forest-certification scheme supported by the leading
environmental organisations, including Greenpeace. Our paper procurement
policy can be found at www.randomhouse.co.uk/environment

Typeset in Sabon LT Std by Palimpsest Book Production Limited,
Falkirk, Stirlingshire

Printed and bound in Great Britain by
Clays Ltd, St Ives plc

THIS SHOULD BE WRITTEN
IN THE PRESENT TENSE

1.

I wrote too much about that step. Where I locked myself out in March. Where I sat and stared in April. Where my mum and dad stood in down jackets well into May, heads at an angle.

The lilacs were in bloom. A bus swung away from the station. A hot smell of diesel, then lilacs again. My arms were bare, the air was warm and mild.

'You forgot these,' said my dad, and handed me the carrier bag. 'We'll head up and wash the place down.'

'Your dad's let them out,' said my mum.

They turned and went back to the car, and my mum got in. A bucket and mop stuck up from the back seat. My dad raised his hand in a wave, his hair lifted in the wind. I went back into the kitchen. I left the door open behind me. I poured a glass of milk and heard them drive away. This is how it might have been.

I'd spent most of the night packing and sorting. Now my good clothes were in the tartan suitcase on the kitchen floor, I'd thrown the rest out. I filled three black bin bags. I was amazed at where it all came from. I couldn't remember having bought that much stuff. There were T-shirts and tops, and all kinds of leggings. Shoes and boots. Unworn dresses from the charity shop.

In one of the bin bags was my so-called work. I never used to think I could throw anything out that I'd put down in words, now I'd got the better of it. I tried not to look, but the odd stiff sentence kept jumping out at me. I glanced away, binning those texts was still hard. In general, I wrote too much about moving house. Like now, the suitcase on the kitchen floor, the carrier bag with my trousers in it on the windowsill. Outside by the road the lilacs bloomed white, and my mum and dad were in a car with a bucket and a mop, already far from Glumsø.

2.

I'd rented the house the year before. It was a bungalow right by the railway line. Dorte paced out the distance in her white clogs while I stood in the front garden and bit into an apple. The landlady had said to help ourselves and pulled down a branch as the three o'clock came in. She was in a trouser suit and looked uncomfortable. It struck me that we were about the same age, twenty or so. She took an apple too, and kept polishing it on her trousers.

'Do you work here?' she said.

'No. I've started studying in Copenhagen,' I said, and cringed at my accent. That trouser suit did nothing for her, the sleeves didn't have enough room for her arms.

'You're well situated here, then.'

'That was what I thought.'

'What are you studying?' she said, and looked towards the road from where Dorte came clacking with the wind in her highlights. 'I think your mum's got her answer now.'

'Twenty-seven metres, give or take,' Dorte said in a loud voice and lifted one foot in the air.

'She's my auntie,' I said.

'Oh, I see,' said the landlady.

She said we could stay as long as we liked, all we had to do was shut the door behind us. We sat on the cracked paintwork on the windowsills in the front room and discussed the rent. I would just about be able to manage without having to borrow. There was a funny smell coming from the bathroom, it reminded me of stagnant pond. Dorte lit a cigarette, she always kept the lighter in the packet.

'It's a lovely house,' she said.

'But I haven't got any furniture.'

'You can have my chest of drawers. And the bumhole lamp, if you like?'

'What I really need is a table.'

'Didn't you see that one in the shed?'

'Here, you mean?'

'Yes, just behind the door,' she said, jumping down.

It was a little kitchen table with hinged leaves. Dorte nodded, her cigarette hanging from the corner of her mouth.

'I can just see that by the window in the front room, can't you?'

'I'll need some curtains.'

'Never mind curtains, you can always get blinds. Look at that,' she said, and pointed at a coffee tin on the shelf, but then a goods train went by and distracted us. We stood in the doorway watching the long line of rust-red wagons.

Before we left, we had a walk round the garden. Besides the apple tree there were pears and mirabelle plums, and a wilderness at the far end that Dorte said was probably full of raspberries. We looked in through all the windows. The place was nice and bright inside, the afternoon sun slanted in across the floors. Dorte pressed her forehead against the kitchen window.

'Those units just need shining up. Original Vordingborg, that is.'

Then she turned round and picked the grass and squashed yellow plum off one clog, then the other. She wiped her hands with some leaves and looked at her watch.

'Take care, love. I'm expecting a pig.'

Two days later I'd moved in. It was a Friday. Dorte drove my boxes and furniture over in the van. She'd given me the old TV she kept as a spare, and the plastic chairs. Late in the afternoon, I took the table apart and carried it into the front room. I screwed the legs back on, it was a tricky manoeuvre turning it upright again. I dragged it over to the window and sat down. If I leaned forward I could see the station at the end of the road. On the other side by the crossing there was the hair salon and a bit further on the pub. I wondered when would be the right time to make some dinner. I'd bought crispy pancakes with chicken on offer. I'd bought flour, too, and spices and cleaning products, it was all still on the worktop in the kitchen. I thought I ought to put shelf liner down in the cupboards and wrote it on a piece of paper: *shelf liner*. I sat at the table until the sun left the room. When I decided to do the pancakes the oven didn't work. The lamp was on, but the oven was stone cold. I still didn't have a frying pan, so I heated them up in a saucepan. They were soggy and burned at the same time. I stood by the worktop and ate them. I'd been hoping they might stretch until the next day. Afterwards I had to lie down. I lay on the floor in the front room, on the frayed carpet. I'd tried to pull it up earlier on, but it seemed to be glued to the floor, the rubber underneath stayed behind.

The window was ajar and I felt the cool evening air in my face. It smelled of beefburgers and something fermented, apples and plums. Cheerful voices came from the main street along with a chinking of bottles. A train arrived, brakes squealing as it drew to a halt. Then silence for a moment, and the doors opened. After that, silence again. A single voice laughed. The blast of a whistle, doors slamming shut, creaking coaches as the engine pulled heavily away. I nearly said cast off.

4.

My dad was given the tartan suitcase as a present when
he finished his apprenticeship. It had been all the way to
Hobro once. I borrowed it the second time I moved away
from home. I'd got a job as an au pair in Vestsjælland
looking after two kids and a golden retriever. I was eighteen.
I was supposed to do the cleaning as well, Mondays,
Wednesdays and Fridays. I only did the Monday and
Wednesday then got a bus home again, the suitcase sliding
around on the floor between the seats. I saw a corn field
outside Havrebjerg.

After that the suitcase lived in my room. At one point
it was a bedside table, the lamp threw a white cone of light
on it all day long. I lay on the bed doing old crosswords
with a biro. I didn't have that many jobs to do, but I had
to remember to turn my jeans inside out when I put them
in the laundry bin.

In the afternoons I'd go for a walk. I walked further and

further along the road before turning back. I came across Per Finland a lot, he didn't know what to do with himself either. He spent the days driving about on his uncle's mini loader and smoking Prince 100s. He'd joined the Young Socialists by mistake, he'd only gone to a party at someone's house in Sandby. I started going home with him. He had a waterbed, it pitched and sloshed. His parents pottered about in the garden below. They couldn't keep the weeds under control, they were both of them teachers. When it was time for me to go his mum would be doing her marking in the front room. One day she came out into the hall and said goodbye. Her hair parted like a pair of curtains.

'I'm so glad you and Per have started seeing each other,' she said.

I didn't know what to say, I couldn't stop thinking about her hair.

'Thanks,' I said, and she nodded a couple of times. I hadn't pulled my socks up properly in my boots, they bunched up under the arches of my feet.

'Mind how you go,' she said, and nodded again, then she went back to her marking.

The yard was covered in slippery sycamore leaves. I walked home over the fields, my boots got heavier and heavier. On Tuesdays and Thursdays Dorte came for dinner if she didn't have a bloke on the go. The meat was always her treat.

5.

The first night in the house I slept sitting up. I sat in the armchair with my legs up and the duvet on top of me. I hadn't put the sheets on the bed, though Dorte had reminded me about it.

'Remember to put your sheets on first thing. You're always knackered after a move.'

Apart from that the bed was assembled and ready, it took up nearly the whole room. I could only just get the door open. By the time I got my head down it was almost midnight. I lay there for ages staring into the dark. There was nothing to see. Eventually I got up and went into the front room, switched on the lamp and sat down in the armchair. I sat quite still and listened. There was nothing to hear either. I reached into my canvas bag on the floor and found a packet of chewing gum, took four pieces and chewed. What a racket it made. I stopped and listened. I chewed until the flavour was gone, then after that I went into the kitchen with the lump. When I opened the bin the vacuum cleaner fell over behind me with a loud clatter. The noise was still ringing in my ears when I sat down in the chair again. I wrapped myself in the duvet and fell asleep with my head hanging down, and slept until a goods train a mile long passed through when morning came. The lamp was still on as the sun came up.

6.

I sat at the drop-leaf table thinking about the word bleary.
It was Saturday morning, I felt like I ought to be doing
something. Finishing the unpacking and taking the empty
boxes out into the shed, for instance, or having a bath.
Fresh air would do me good as well, I could at least go
over the road and walk down the little path by the flats
to the supermarket, buy some vegetables and some apples
for the train that coming week. I thought about my savings
account. It had lasted nearly three years, but now it was
almost empty. There was only about four thousand kroner
left. Then I realised I was looking out at my own apple
tree. I blurted something out in surprise, got up from the
chair and stuck my clogs on. I picked four big green apples
and put them down on the step. Around the back I discovered a clothes line strung out between the two pear trees,
but there were no pears on the branches. The leaves had
big brown patches on them, or else they were turning

yellow and red. I remembered I needed to renew my rail-card and fetched my purse from the front room.

An elderly man on a bike was posting a letter outside the station, he straddled the crossbar with one foot on the ground as he dropped it in the box. Upstairs on the first floor the windows were open, music was streaming out and a hand appeared with a duster in it. I pushed the door open and went into the ticket office. The guy behind the counter looked up from his roll with crumbs stuck to his lips.

'Hi.'

'I'm interrupting your breakfast.'

'Sorry.'

He chewed and swallowed as he smiled. His hair was fair and quite long. I wondered how he'd ended up in that ticket office. There was a newspaper open on the desk, on top of it a book about Pink Floyd with a bookmark sticking out.

There was a bit of trouble with my railcard because I belonged in a different zone now, he had to do me a new one. I still had a photo left from the booth, unfortunately not my best. I put it on the counter in front of him along with the money. He stapled it in and folded the plastic wallet, then handed it over. He was smiling the whole time.

'You can catch the next one if you hurry,' he said as I turned to leave.

'It's Saturday today,' I said. I could feel his eyes following me on my way out.

Outside, the music from upstairs now mingled with the sound of a vacuum cleaner. For some reason I hurried over to the platform. It was deserted. The train came rumbling through the trees and began to brake. I covered my ears. The doors opened in front of me and a tall guy got off with a rucksack, he was having a job with it. The guard leaned out at the front end with his whistle in his mouth and his eyes fixed on his left wrist. He looked up at me and made a big sweeping gesture towards the train. At first I shook my head, but then when he did it again and blew his whistle I got on anyway. I scampered up the two steps and stood for a moment by the open door as the train pulled slowly away, then I jumped back down onto the platform again. I landed awkwardly and twisted my knee. The train was hardly moving but it was still a fall. Nevertheless, I sprang quickly to my feet. I went back over the tracks and gave the station building a wide berth. I'd torn a hole in my jeans, the new ones. I hadn't even shut my front door, the place was wide open. I mimicked the guard's gesture as I cut through the garden. I don't know what got into me.

Because the house had been left open in the short time I'd been at the station, on the platform, on the train and on the platform again, I went and looked in all the rooms. I looked behind the doors, inside the cupboards and under the bed. I looked in the shed, too, and behind the oil tank on my way back inside. I did it casually, like there was nothing the matter, as if I was looking for a lost ball or a garden tool.

Afterwards I sat down in the armchair in the front room with a needle and thread and tried to mend my jeans. I was no good at it. I put the TV on and watched a gardening programme and later on the football while I ate most of a packet of biscuits. Towards evening I fell asleep in the chair, my head kept nodding to one side. Eventually, I lay down on the floor and slept there far too long, clutching a cushion with my mouth half open. My throat was parched when I woke up in the dark several hours later, but it could have been the biscuits. Now I wouldn't be able to fall asleep at bedtime, again. All I could do was sit and doodle and listen to late-night radio until it turned into breakfast radio and a heavy goods train came thundering by. Thirty-four wagons in all, Transwaggon, Transwaggon. I put my head on the table and closed my eyes, watching lines turn into oblongs and rectangles behind my eyelids.

7

From Per Finland's waterbed you could see the road weave between fields and farms and tatty cottages. Thin coils of smoke rose up from all the houses. When we opened the window we could smell the birch wood from the chimney. Per laughed and ran a rough finger down my back. His voice was rough too, he kept clearing his throat. We had electric panel heaters at ours, we were waiting for central heating. But after she moved from Slaglille, Dorte got a wood-burning stove, she used milk cartons packed tight with newspaper. I put our own cartons aside for her. We couldn't give her that many, but she had an arrangement with a canteen and another for old newspapers. In Per's house they kept *Politiken* and a sports weekly. It was Per's job to check the letter box in the driveway. He wrapped his long arms around me in bed one Saturday afternoon. I'd been up early and had gone for a walk. We bumped into each other at the T-junction after the pond, he was out walking too. The lanes were covered in mud from the fields.

'Let's go home and take our clothes off,' he said and put his hand in mine. We traipsed along the verge side by side in our wellies.

From the window all the fields were brown and black, the woods had lost the last of their colour too. Some crows took off one after another as a minibus came down from the main road. His body was warm to snuggle up to, he had good circulation. I liked the way his eyebrows tensed when he was enjoying it most, his face collapsed above me. Then the crows landed one by one. After a bit they were all together on the road again, striding about and pecking.

'Are your mum and dad in?' I asked.

'No, they're at a do.'

'At this time of day?'

'A lunch.'

'Oh, right.'

'They won't be back for hours.'

'Do they teach at the same school?'

'No, they didn't want to. It'd be asking for trouble.'

'Yeah, I suppose it would.'

'But that's not where the lunch is.'

'Where?'

'At one of the schools.'

'Oh, right.'

'It's at the beekeepers' association.'

'I didn't know you had bees.'

'We don't. Only the ones that happen by. It's years since we had bees, they're too much work.'

'Oh, I see.'

He took a very long shower. I lay listening to him as the water rushed in the pipes. Every now and then he groaned with satisfaction. I wondered if he would have done the same if I hadn't been there. I got out of bed and put my trousers and top on, steam billowed from the bathroom. He stood with his eyes closed under the shower. I sat on the narrow windowsill and leaned my head against the pane. They still had last year's Christmas tree on the patio, it didn't have a needle left. It looked like it had been a Norway spruce. Eventually, the water stopped. He turned to get his towel and smiled at me across the room in surprise.

'Are you up and dressed?'

'It was only for a minute,' I said.

As we lay in bed again a bit later, the Volvo rumbled across the cobbles in the yard. Per's parents came tramping cheerfully into the house, and after a bit the smell of coffee rose up through the floorboards. We went down and joined them. Much, much later that same evening we had lamb shank in the kitchen, all four of us. I'd had lamb once before at Dorte's, a funeral lamb instead of Halkidiki. She'd just ditched her removal man, they were supposed to have gone there together. In the end it was only the two of us. There was a side salad of cucumber and feta. We sat for a long time just looking at it all.

'What appetites we've not got!' she said and lit a cigarette. She'd been on the sunbeds for a fortnight at Health & Beauty just to be ready. Her voice and colour were from different worlds.

8.

After lunch on the Sunday I had a burst of efficiency despite being tired. I hadn't slept properly for two nights by then. I lugged my dirty washing in a bin bag along the main street towards the church, then down a little hill to a corner where I was sure there was a launderette, only there wasn't. There wasn't even a corner, just a patch of grass with a sandpit and a swing. Two girls were sitting on a bench smoking, they'd never heard of any launderette. One of them said there was a tailor's where they did dry-cleaning. She had new white pumps on and got the other girl to stamp out her cigarette. The other girl thought there might be a launderette by a block of flats in Sorø. She wouldn't swear on it, but she was fairly sure. It was because her uncle lived in Sorø. As they spoke I realised I didn't have any change. I'd used it all up paying for my railcard the day before. I trudged back up the little hill past the old merchant's house and along the main street. The bookshop window was decked out with magazines and woolly socks, apparently the socks were knitted by a local woman. They were striped and came in all different sizes. I'd been in on the Friday to buy some fine-tipped marker pens. The woman asked if I meant *fell-tips*. She laid out a selection on the counter and I bought two so as not to look stingy.

I carried the bin bag slung over my shoulder. It was heavy, full of towels and trousers and tops, colours the lot of it. I'd imagined there was enough for two loads. Now I went home and filled the bath with hot water and soap powder. I emptied the bin bag into the water and separated the clothes with a big wooden spoon, then left it all to soak.

In the front room I emptied a removal box and put the contents away in the drawers and at the bottom of the wardrobe in the bedroom. I made myself a cup of coffee and drank it standing up by the worktop in the kitchen, then I went and rinsed the clothes and wrung them out. It was hard work, especially the jeans. My hands were bright red and my knuckles all sore by the time I stood at the clothes line with the washing in an old tub I'd found in the shed. It was a bit dirty, but it couldn't be helped. There was just enough room on the clothes line if I hung everything by the narrow end. I had one big bath towel and two small fawn-coloured ones with an advert for some coffee on them. I went into the shed and tidied up a bit, stacked some old flowerpots so they took up half the space, threw a pile of damp newspapers in the bin. The sky was very dark. Afterwards, as I stood with another cup of coffee in the kitchen, it began to rain. Just a bit at first, but then in no time it was lashing against the windows. I dashed out into the garden and snatched the washing from the line and dumped the lot in the utility room.

Later that afternoon I hung the clothes over all the chairs, the chest of drawers and the radiator, and turned the heating on full. The front room filled with the smell of fabric softener and I opened the window a bit. I went and lay down on the bed and pulled the duvet up over my head. When I woke up it was getting dark. I went to the bathroom and brushed my teeth. As I stood there with my mouth full of toothpaste, there was a knock on the door. It was a young couple in raincoats with an empty picnic basket. They wanted to know if they could use the phone.

'There's one over there,' I said and nodded towards the station.

'It's out of order,' said the girl. 'That's why we're asking.'

'We forgot to get off the train at Lundby, we only need to get a message to her brother. He's waiting for us,' said the guy.

'But I haven't got a telephone. I've only just moved in.'

'So has he. That's why we forgot to get off. Not here,

like,' said the girl and scratched her thigh. She was wearing white jeans with grass stains on.

'Oh,' I said.

'We think it's because it hasn't been emptied,' he said. 'Anyway, soggy to bother you.'

The girl laughed and shook her head at him. She lifted up the basket apologetically.

'We've been at Knuthenborg Safari Park since ten this morning.'

'Perhaps you can ask the people who live above the station,' I said. 'I know someone lives there.'

'We will. Thanks a lot for your help,' they said almost at the same time, and stepped down onto the path. They turned and waved, raincoats standing out in the fading light.

I didn't know what to do with myself. I felt I should wash my hair. I realised I hadn't had my dinner. I went into the kitchen and opened all the cupboards. There was some pasta and pitta bread and several cans of tuna, but nothing I really fancied. I went into the front room and looked across at the station. There was a light on upstairs, but I couldn't see anyone there. I stuffed a hundred-krone note in my pocket together with my front-door key, pulled on a jumper and shut the door behind me.

The snack bar was a sausage stand with a wooden extension, in the car park next to the baker's. I bought a hamburger and some chips and carried the box home in both hands with steam coming out of the holes in the lid. As I got to the house I saw a young woman come out of my front garden and walk slowly back in the direction of the station. She stopped and pulled her sleeves down over her hands and glanced back towards the house. She straightened up and folded her arms as soon as she saw me. I didn't know whether to say hello or not. I turned up the path with my takeaway, but then she hurried over.

'Hey, excuse me.'

She had wet hair and a shrill voice.

'It's not on, you know, sending people over to ours to use the phone.'

'No, I'm sorry,' I said.

'We can't have people knocking on the door thinking they can just come in and make a call whenever it suits them, they can go to the petrol station instead.'

'I really am sorry.'

'Or the one by the church. It's only a little walk, if they really need to call someone.'

'Of course.'

'Besides, I was in the middle of something,' she said, gathering her oversized jumper around her.

'I'm really sorry.'

'Well, then.'

She nodded, then turned and went back towards the station. On the step under the lamp the young couple with the picnic basket stood looking across at me. The girl waved. I lifted my takeaway to wave back, the girl said something to her boyfriend, then they came towards me. I sent them a bewildered look I thought could be seen from a distance, but before I knew it they were standing there in front of me, and the girl was all smiles.

'It's so nice of you, really,' she said.

9.

So there I sat in the front room with my chips and this young couple, surrounded by all my washing. I'd left the hamburger on the worktop in the kitchen. They both sat on the edge of their chairs, the girl jiggled her foot up and down, the table kept trembling. Perhaps I hadn't tightened the screws properly, it felt a bit rickety.

'Help yourselves,' I said.

'Thanks,' said her boyfriend without taking any.

'Our train's at twenty past ten,' said the girl.

He looked at his watch.

'Exactly one hour and fifty minutes.'

'Did you get hold of your brother?' I said.

'Yes. He was supposed to pick us up in Lundby,' said the girl.

'Yes, you said,' I said, and she nodded.

'He's only just moved there. We're from Sundbyvester

actually. All of us, I mean,' she said, jiggling away. The whole table was shaking.

'All three of you?' I said.

'Four, actually. He's got a boy aged two,' said her boyfriend.

'What a lot of you,' I said.

'We were going to see his new house on the way back. But now we're just going to go home,' she said.

'Your foot, love,' he said, and she smiled. She had such a nice smile, then after that we were quiet for a bit.

The Hamburg express came thundering through. I'd eaten less than a quarter of the chips, the boyfriend had eaten one.

'You forgot your hamburger,' the girl said to me.

'Oh, yes. Do you want it?'

'No, you have it. We've eaten loads today, we're not at all hungry.'

'Me neither.'

'You can take it with you for your lunch tomorrow,' said the guy.

'What sort of job do you do?' said the girl.

'I'm a student. In Copenhagen.'

'Really? Handy living here, then.'

'Yes, it is,' I said, and they both nodded. They were leaning slightly over the table with their hands in their laps.

They told me about their trip to Knuthenborg and all the animals they'd seen. They went there once a year, his aunt lived near Nakskov and they always went in her car. It was an Opel registered for commercial use, she had a domestic cleaning business. Normally they went in the summer, but his aunt had broken her wrist falling down a slope at Nakskov Fjord, she thought she'd seen a man she knew. It was a complicated fracture, they didn't even discover it for a few days. She'd got poorly and had to stay in bed with her arm full of fluid. People kept ringing to ask when she was coming to do their cleaning. Eventually she managed to drive to Stokkemarke and do the floors in two bungalows. Her arm was in plaster for six weeks, she couldn't do a thing with it afterwards. She'd only just started driving again, which was why their trip to Knuthenborg had been put off.

'She lost a lot of customers while she was off sick,' he said.

'She's eight per cent invalid now, but she can't do without her hand,' said the girl.

'Who can?' he said and they both nodded. After that we were quiet again for a bit.

'What do you do, anyway?' I asked.

'We've got summer jobs in the Tivoli Gardens,' he said. 'I sell snacks and she's on Hook-a-Duck.'

'That's how we met, two years and three months ago. I can hardly believe it,' she said, and he ruffled her hair.

'You got hooked yourself.'

'Ha, ha,' she said and ruffled back. Then she cleared her throat. 'No, really. Tivoli's the best job in the world. There's no two days alike.'

'Shame about the rest of the year, though,' he said, and she gave him a shove.

'Ha, ha, ha.'

We decided to watch TV. I had three channels, but there was nothing on. Even so, we ended up watching a programme about silent movies. She snuggled up to him and put her head on his shoulder, I could tell she was struggling to stay awake. When the programme finished I got up.

'We'd best get to the train in good time,' I said.

'Are you going to walk us over? Thanks ever so much,' said the girl. They jumped to their feet and got into their muddy trainers. There was still plenty of time as we said goodbye on the platform. I waved again when I crossed over the tracks. They waved back, then he found something in his raincoat pocket that distracted them. I sneaked a look at the timetable on the board. It was Sunday and there were no more trains. They realised the same thing a moment later and caught me up on my front path looking sheepish. I put the key in the door and the girl put a hand on my shoulder and thanked me for being so kind. I answered without turning round.

'It's nothing, really.'

'Oh, but it is,' she said.

'We can lie on our raincoats in the front room,' he said.

'There's carpet in there,' said the girl. 'The coats will do for covers.'

'I've got some old blankets somewhere.'

'We can all go in together in the morning,' said the girl. 'What time's your train? We'll sit quiet, I promise.'

'If there's something you need to read or something, she means.'

'Just after nine,' I said.

10.

I slept soundly that night. I didn't hear a peep from the couple in the front room, or from the trains, or the boiler in the utility room next door. It must have kicked in during the night, the place was sweltering when I woke up. My cheeks felt like they were on fire. It was light outside and the sky was blue. I stared emptily at the bark of the old pear tree for a minute, then came another gentle knock on the door and after a second it opened.

'Morning,' whispered the girl. 'Just to say it's half past eight.'

She was already in her raincoat and her boyfriend was standing behind her with his round, smiling face.

'I hope you don't mind, but we made some coffee. Here you go,' he said, handing me a mug. I jumped out of bed in my nightshirt.

'Thanks.'

'We weren't sure whether to wake you earlier. We

thought you might be the kind of person who got ready in no time.'

'That's all right,' I said, and took a slurp. It was really strong. They stood watching me.

'Sorry, I'm still half asleep,' I said.

'We'll just wait outside in the garden,' said the girl.

'It's a lovely sunny day, it's not often we get the chance to drink coffee outside in the mornings. Anyway, like she said, it's only half eight,' he said.

I could hear them talking in the front garden while I got dressed and tried to do my hair in the hall mirror. I felt hot and drowsy. They spoke in turn, but I couldn't pick out the words. Once, I lay on a beach all day with the muffled voices of strangers all around me. Later I thought it had been so blissful lying there unnoticed in a hum of conversation. My hair wouldn't do what I wanted, it stuck out on the side I'd slept on. I patted it down with some water and gathered it in a loose ponytail, then I got my leather jacket and went into the front room for my bag and a book. All the washing had been folded up in a neat pile on the table. The radiator was still on full blast, I turned it down and picked up my key from the chest of drawers, then went outside.

'Was it five past nine it was due?' said the girl, and I nodded.

'Yes. Have you got tickets?'

'No, we need to get some. Have you got enough money, Lasse?' she said, and he had, at least almost, they only needed to borrow forty kroner when we got to the station. The train was on time but crowded. We went all the way through from one end to the other, but there were only two seats free that were next to each other.

'You take it,' she said to me. 'I'll sit on his knee.'

So I sat down by the window, Lasse sat beside me with her on his lap. Their raincoats rustled every time they moved. He blew her hair away from his face. I reached into my bag for my book, opened it, then stared out at the reddening fringe of a wood and some gulls flocking in the fields. A bit later there were rooks and geese, a blue tractor left at a boundary with its door open and a man on his knees in the furrow. I saw him get up and shake his head in resignation, and then we'd gone past. After that nothing, then Ringsted's array of rooftops.

11.

Per Finland's mum was called Ruth, she edited a little periodical. She'd been allowed to use her school's copying facilities. Teachers and pupils and other people could have poems and short stories published in it. She sat at the table surrounded by sheets of paper and was in a quandary, a woodwork teacher had written a fairy tale in verse about Hans Christian Andersen. It wasn't dreadful, but it wasn't good enough to be included either. The periodical was even called *The Duckling* and she'd got the idea for it during the big flu epidemic the year before. She patted the seat of the chair next to her. I got up from the sofa and went and sat down beside her.

'Do you write poems?' she said.

'No, not really.'

'You should. Per says you're good at writing.'

'She is as well,' said Per from the sofa, slouching down. His fringe had grown, it got in the way of his eyelashes every now and then.

'You should read the song lyrics she wrote for her aunt's birthday,' he said.

'How old was she?'

'Only forty-three,' I said.

'Go on, then,' she said, and so I cleared my throat and began to sing. My voice was shaky, I had to pause between two verses to clear my throat again. The way I sang made it more serious than it was meant to be. Ruth sat with her head tilted to one side, Per sat up. Just as I finished, the door of the study opened and his dad was standing there with a recorder in his mouth.

'Not now, Hans-Jakob,' said Ruth. She leaned back in her chair and smiled at me.

'It's a lovely song. I'd like to publish it.'

'Isn't it a bit private?' I said.

'No, that doesn't matter.'

'It's a party song, isn't it?' said Hans-Jakob.

'For her aunt,' said Per.

'When's the party?'

'A while ago. Or rather, there wasn't one,' I said.

'It was just the two of them,' said Per.

In the evening we had red wine from Spain with our stew. We sat at the table in the kitchen and talked for ages. The fire roared in the stove and we laughed at the woodwork teacher's verse. Per stretched his legs out under the table and put mine in a scissor lock. It was almost midnight. Ruth went into the pantry and improvised a dessert out of preserved apricots and nut brittle. Hans-Jakob opened a bottle of dessert wine and the thought occurred to me: I'm an adult, I've been a dinner guest. I was nineteen years old and the moon was out above the stable. A couple of weeks later I moved in there with Per, into the new bedsit they'd had converted on the first floor, with its own bathroom. It was the third time I'd left home. My mum and dad gave us a pewter mug as a moving-in present, but they never got the chance to see the place.

12.

The first time I left home I moved in with Dorte. I was in my second year at the gymnasium school, it had been a harsh winter. Every day I cycled two kilometres the back way along the lane between the fields to the bus stop. My wet hair froze into icicles. I got the bus to Næstved station, from there a city bus ran every twenty minutes. Dorte thought it was too hard on me. She'd got herself a two-bedroom flat with a balcony in the centre of Næstved.

In the mornings when I got up the coffee maker was all ready. She wrote me notes on the filter, and put my mug out on a tray along with butter and jam. I made toast and sat down in the living room, I didn't need to get going until the last minute. Sometimes she'd get stuck with the crossword and leave it for me, her pencil lying like a half-smoked cigarette in the ashtray. In the evenings we played charades.

Dorte's efforts had us in stitches, we laughed so much the downstairs neighbour phoned to complain.

'Yes, all right, you miserable old bat,' said Dorte, almost before she'd put down the receiver, and then we reached for the blankets and laughed hysterically into the wool until it set our teeth on edge.

Dorte was convinced that she was the one who had introduced fake fur coats to mid and southern Sjælland. She'd had four at one stage, but the pink one was worn out and she'd given the long one away to a homeless person. I got the one with Mickey Mouse on it. We stood in her bedroom in front of the mirror.

'You can have it, it suits you,' she said. 'If you haven't worn it for a year get rid, that's what I say.'

'Are you sure?'

'Funeral outfits excepted.'

I did another twirl by the mirror, but then the doorbell rang, and it was my mum. She'd been to the ear, nose and throat specialist and now she was stopping by with a couple of books she thought I might have forgotten. She'd had her hair done, too, Dorte complimented her on it. We stood for a bit in the hall. They couldn't find a parking space, my dad was waiting outside. I hadn't missed the books, and my mum didn't mention the fur coat. Dorte didn't say anything about the car park round the back either, but she had to be getting back to the shop, she'd only popped home for an hour.

I wasn't keen on that coat. I wore my old woollen one instead, and hung the fur outside on the balcony so it would be wet with snow when Dorte came home at six. When the front door opened a smell of fried onions filled the air. She put the food in the oven to warm and changed into her jogging pants, then drew her legs up underneath her on the sofa next to me.

'Don't you wear it much?' she said.

'Not really.'

'Tell you what, we'll give it to Vagn's sister. I think it's more her style.'

I hadn't heard about Vagn before, but he came round that same evening. He had funny teeth, and a month later Dorte gave up the lease. I moved back home in the middle of April, the woods were starred with thimbleweed. I biked along the track behind the lane in the late afternoons with my bag on the pannier rack. Everything smelled of soil and sprouting plants, and my mum and dad waved hello from wherever they happened to be in the garden. We never mentioned Dorte all summer. I cycled out to see her in Skelby on the sly and bought new potatoes to take with me from a stall by the road. Vagn lay at her feet on the patio with a cigarette protruding from his front teeth. The potatoes made me feel stupid.

But then autumn and winter came, and before I'd left school Dorte was back in our kitchen on Tuesdays and Thursdays, my mum at the worktop with her back to us, endlessly stirring a pot with some utensil or other.

13.

The sky over Copenhagen Central was bright blue. We went up the steps at the far end of the platform and shook hands on Tietgensgade. I clutched the collar of my leather jacket tight, there was an icy wind coming from somewhere. The girl shivered too, her eyes were watering and her hair was getting blown all over the place.

'Thanks ever so much,' she said, and Lasse joined in:

'Yes, it was so nice of you.'

'Take care of yourself. Which way are you going?' she said, and I pointed. They were going that way too. We walked to the crossing and waited for the green man. A number 12 pulled away from the stop over the road in a cloud of diesel fumes.

'Bad luck,' she said, then the light changed and we stepped onto the crossing, my bag kept slipping off my shoulder. A car was turning and gave way for us. Another driver blew his horn and someone shouted. My ponytail blew into my face and then we were out of the wind, sheltered by of the building on the corner. We all stopped at the bus stop.

'Are you getting this one too?' asked the girl. I shook my head.

'No, normally I walk.'

'We do that normally as well today,' said Lasse and patted the pocket of his raincoat.

'Is it the university you go to? Out in Amager?' asked the girl. I nodded and we set off again, the three of us together, she let him walk in front and stuck by my side.

'In that case we can see you to the door. It's exactly the way we're going.'

Lasse led the way over pedestrian crossings and round street corners, across Langebro Bridge and down a flight of steps on the other side. He stood at the bottom and threw out his arms.

'Islands Brygge, ladies.'

We came past the supermarket on Njalsgade. She said they'd once found a hair elastic in a packet of mince they'd bought there. To make amends, the manager had given them a whole economy pack with five kilos of pork and a bunch of roses to go with it, so all in all they'd done well out of it. Of course, the hair elastic was a bit unpleasant, it was one of those glittery ones, it had turned up in one of Lasse's meatballs. For a while afterwards they made a point of looking for things wrong with their shopping. They'd found a wasp in a jar of marmalade too. We were almost there now, the Amager campus was just off to the right. When we got to the bike stands I was about to say goodbye, but Lasse shook his head and walked me right up to the entrance, pulled one of the doors and held it open for me.

'Have a nice day. And thanks again for all your help.'

'It was lovely meeting you,' said the girl, and stepped forward to give me a little hug. Two young guys with leather shoulder bags went past and left a smell of musk behind them. They breezed in through Lasse's open door.

'I'd better go,' I said.

'Best of luck with everything.'

'Same to you.'

'Thanks.'

'Bye, then,' I said, and went in. Lasse let go of the door and it closed. I went over to the noticeboards and stood there for a bit. My nose was running, I searched for a hankie in my bag but couldn't find one. I went to the toilets, and a girl with a diagonal fringe nodded to me before turning back to her lipstick. I blew my nose, looked at myself in the mirror and went out again. I opened a door at the entrance. They were gone. I scurried out into the wind, turned onto Artillerivej and walked back towards town clutching the collar of my leather jacket again with one hand. My bag kept slipping off my shoulder and I ended up putting the strap over my head. Cyclists rang their bells, a bus braked hard and accelerated again almost at once. To the right, under the bridge, a tall, thin girl stepped out of her clothes and jumped into the water to loud shrieking and whooping. Another girl stood with a camera and a towel ready. The wind gusted and cut to the bone.

I bought a roll and a cup of coffee at the bakery in the arcade. The place was expensive, but you could sit there as long as you liked and they didn't charge for water. I sat right at the back against the wall. I got my book out and tried to read. After almost an hour I went to Scala. I went round the different floors looking at jewellery and jeans, I took the escalator up to the cinema, but there was nothing on that I wanted to see. Before I went home I bought a melon in the Irma supermarket. I sat on the train with it in my canvas bag, looking out at back gardens and sheds and little houses. I thought about my own bungalow with the apple tree and no curtains. It was a very sad melon. I put it in the window in the kitchen, it stayed there until well into November.

14.

Per set the alarm every night, and every morning we over-slept. It was broad daylight by the time we woke up entwined. I extricated myself and got out of bed. His parents had long since gone to work. A pheasant strutted about in the yard, it flapped its wings and flew up onto the bird table with a loud squawk. Some sparrows sat like little inflated puffballs in the bushes. I told Per:

'Come and look at the sparrows. They're all inflated.'

'So am I after last night,' he said and came up behind me. He put his arms around my waist and I leaned my head back against his shoulder.

'The prawn nibbles were nice,' I said.

I'd started wearing woolly socks, Ruth had given me a pair from Abracadabra. She'd bought us a hammock as well, it hung from the beams in the bedsit and was full of our dirty washing. Per rummaged around in it looking for a T-shirt. He'd have a ponytail soon.

'Do you fancy going to the sports hall today?' he said.

'And do what?'

'Play badminton. There's always a court free on Mondays.'

'You don't want to play against me.'

'Yes, I do.'

'I can't, anyway. I've got to go to work.'

'Oh, yeah, I forgot. I'll go with you then.'

'You don't have to.'

'I can sit and wait for you outside.'

'It's much too cold today.'

'I'll take a ball with me. Or I can go in and play with one of the kids.'

'You're not allowed.'

'Yes, I am.'

Ruth had got me a job twice a week at the recreation club at her school. I helped a little boy called Niller with his homework. I saw him on Mondays and Wednesdays at two o'clock, just as the other kids and the staff sat down to their fruit and biscuits. Niller flew into a temper every time, he'd get up from the table with his fists clenched and his little shoulders trembling. It wasn't the best start for homework, but the job was from two until three and that was that. We sat in a little room among cushions and board games, with his books in front of us. There was a musty smell of unwashed hair, packed lunches and dried-up mud. I got decent money for it. I told Ruth I'd pay for my keep, but all she did was roll her eyes. The job had been Per's for a week and a half before I started, but he couldn't teach when it came to maths, he had to open the little window in the cushion room and swear under his breath while Niller sat stiff as a board behind him with his maths book. As soon as my first wages came in I went to the flower shop near the school and bought Ruth a big cactus. She was pleased and put it on the floor next to the spinning wheel.

Per went with me to work and back again, he tickled me on the waterbed until I nearly fainted, he took his clothes off and put them back on again several times a day, went with me to the doctor's when I got pregnant and on the bus to the hospital seven long days later, and on the way back that same afternoon he'd got me a present, a hair slide from a silversmith, made out of a spoon with a proper hallmark. I was so relieved and felt so much better despite the anaesthetic, we couldn't stop laughing until the driver told us to be quiet. But then in the evening I had to go and lie down before dinner. Per told his parents I was feeling a bit off colour. He came over with some smørrebrød a bit later, meticulously trimmed with cress and jellied stock, he'd made such an effort. He ran his hand up and down my back, and put a glass of milk on my bedside table.

One day we went for a long walk. We went through the woods and round the other side by the stream and further on along the winding road. It had been sunny all week, but the nights were still cold. The fields were white. We held hands, except for when a car came, then we'd step onto the verge, where the snow was hard on top and could carry our weight. We stood kissing as two cars drove by, the second one slowed down and pulled in a bit further on. It was my mum and dad. They got out and we walked towards each other. It was the third time they met Per. They shook his hand. He smiled the whole time, his long fringe kept falling down in front of his eyes. He took off a glove and tucked his hair behind his ears, it would have looked better if he'd left it alone. My dad gave me a hug, and my mum stood right up close to me. My dad asked Per if we were keeping warm under the covers. Per kept smiling and messing with his hair. A car went by going too fast, we all had to stand aside in the snow for a minute.

After they'd gone, we walked a good way without speaking, then turned back when we got to the boggy bit.

'Haven't you got a tissue so you can blow your nose?' I said.

'No, I haven't.'

'Can't you use a leaf, then? You keep sniffing all the time.'

'Does it bother you?'

'I wouldn't mention it if it didn't,' I said and could hardly recognise my own voice, I felt like throwing myself flat in a snow drift. Any other time I would have done, and Per would have followed suit within a second. But I kept on at a brisk pace, slightly ahead of him the whole time. At the edge of the woods a buzzard took off from a fence-post right in front of us. We almost felt it in the air, it gave us a fright. That helped, and we began to laugh. A bit later Per took his hand away and left me walking along holding an empty glove. He got me every time, I never learned.

When we got home we made raspberry slices. While we waited for the pastry to chill I did the washing-up from the day before and wiped all the cupboards down with a cloth. They were yellow and blue, Per had painted them himself a few years before. He'd been allowed to choose the colours on his own and after he finished he painted a huge flower on the end wall of the stable. The flower had become a local landmark, you could see it all the way from Aversi.

We ate three slices each, the rest we put on a plate for Ruth and Hans-Jakob. Then we went for a lie-down. We didn't wake up until late evening and couldn't sleep again for hours.

15.

They'd forgotten their picnic basket, it was sticking out under the shrubs in the front garden. I discovered it on the Tuesday morning when I went over to catch the train. I'd tried some new eyeshadow, it was dusty green and supposed to go all the way up, only my eyelids weren't the right shape. It was only a couple of minutes till the train was due, so I left the basket where it was and cut through the station. The guy in the ticket office was busy with a customer.

It was sunny again, but bitterly cold. I wished I'd worn something else instead of my thin trench coat. I'd got it for fifty kroner in a charity shop, there was a business card from a barber's in the pocket. I'd bought a beret as well, but I didn't put it on until after Roskilde. People sat chattering all through the carriage. A school class had reserved the main compartment, the teacher and a couple of the kids were in ours. The sliding door in between kept opening.

'Do we get off at Central, Hanne?'

'We haven't got homework for tomorrow, have we?'

'Have we got time to buy something to drink?'

'Yes, just stay in your seats,' said the teacher, and stood up. She went next door and repeated the instruction, then came back with apologetic eyebrows beneath her school-teacher's fringe.

'There wasn't enough room for us in one compartment.'

'It'd be a bit of a squeeze. Day out in town, is it?' said an elderly man.

'Geological Museum,' she said with a nod and rummaged in her bag. The two kids sent longing looks to their class-mates in the other compartment.

'Øster Voldgade,' said the man, and she nodded again. The man looked across at me.

'It's on Øster Voldgade,' he said, and I nodded as well even though I had no idea, but I knew Albertslundplanen, the housing development we clattered past. I'd been to a so-called reading group there three weeks before. It was the first meeting, there was nothing in particular we were supposed to have read. There were four of us. The girl who lived there was called Margrethe, she wore a beret too. She'd read law to begin with, but that had been a mistake, she'd only chosen the course on political grounds. We had goat's cheese and baguette with red wine, and she made coffee in a French press and heated up the milk. She had a shelving system in untreated pine, and a proper sofa. She was two years older than me. The others were even older, their names were Benny and Hase. Benny was a woman. She had a loud and throaty laugh, smoked Look cigarettes because they were out of Cecils, and pinched off the filter. There was something odd about Hase. He was round-shouldered and the waist of his trousers was too high up. But his face was kind, he sang in the church choir in Greve Landsby. We drank three bottles of wine and decided to call ourselves the Oldies. I left with Hase when it was time to go, it took twenty-one minutes on the S-train. He asked if we could have lunch together the next day in the canteen. He bent forward and kissed me on the hand when we went our separate ways at Central Station. I took his hand without thinking about it and gave it a squeeze, it made him smile. He smiled at me all the way down the escalator to the Nykøbing train. I hadn't been to the reading group since. Maybe there hadn't been any meetings.

I let the school children get off before me, there was a smell of chewing gum in the air around them. I put my head through the strap of my bag and went straight to Rådhuspladsen. There was a branch of Privatbanken on the corner and I took out four hundred kroner. Then I went back and got on a number 12 to the Amager campus, I drank a cup of coffee at the far end of the canteen. I had a piece of cheesecake too, and then I went to the library and wandered round the shelves. I pulled out a guide to

52

punctuation and sat down with it. I looked at the back cover. I looked in the index. I looked at my hands. I tried to pull myself together. I read and took nothing in.

After an hour I got the bus back into town and went round Scala. I bought a scarf and wrapped it round my neck, and stuffed it well down into the opening of my trench coat. I saw three versions of myself in a fitting room, each one stumpier than the next. Then I left the fitting room and went down the stairs and along the street to Central Station, and got on the next train just before two. I was home an hour later. The sun was low behind the supermarket, I picked two apples and put the picnic basket away in the shed.

Late in the afternoon my dad came and picked me up for fried herring, it had been arranged for ages. My mum had made stewed potatoes, she had new, faintly orange lipstick on. She put her hand on my forearm when I reached across for the dish. They'd been out at Jan and Bitte's over the weekend in the trenches, as my dad said, he'd been helping Jan dig a ditch. They'd had fondue, but it hadn't been up to much, all that oil. He asked how my course was going and I said fine. He said fondue might be more my kind of thing. My mum asked about the house, how I was settling in, and if there was anything I needed to borrow.

They drove me home at eight, the two of them together. I insisted on being dropped off by the church for the walk. In the night I lay and stared out into the darkness of the back garden again. It was like the whole house was creaking and groaning: doors, floors, skirting boards and panels.

16.

Dorte was so proud of my song in *The Duckling* she asked for a stack to have on the counter. We sat in the kitchen at the back of the shop with a cup of coffee, her cigarette lay smouldering in the ashtray, she was too busy to smoke it. She laughed and coughed and held up the page in front of her, humming the melody and reading the words over and over again.

'That's lovely, that is. Too good not to be in print,' she said.

'I think it's a bit odd.'

'It is a bit. But nice, all the same.'

'Remember your fag.'

'Oh, I forgot.'

She took a drag, then a couple more puffs before stubbing it out with quick, efficient jabs. Then she got up and lifted the lid off a big pot and a tart smell of apples rose up.

'Do you want some stewed apples?' she asked.

'No, thanks.'

'You'll wither away soon. Aren't they feeding you on the farm?'

'Oh, yes.'

'Is he good to you?'

'Very.'

'Spoil you rotten, does he?'

'Mostly.'

'And you're earning your keep?'

'Yes.'

'Good,' she said, and went out into the shop. When she came back she had two five-hundred krone notes in her hand, she crumpled them up and pressed them into my palm.

'Here. Get yourself a perm.'

'Ha, ha. I can't take this.'

'You can and you will.'

Not long after, I started earning decent money writing lyrics for party songs. To begin with it was just for teachers in the Ringsted area, but then word got round as far as Osted. A single event sometimes meant four songs. I charged a hundred and fifty kroner a piece and could do two in a week, even though I did set myself certain rules. On principle I wouldn't duplicate a line from any song I'd written before, and if I could avoid it I wouldn't rhyme on a verb. I hated the narrative present. I wrote lying down on the waterbed. Ruth gave me a rhyming dictionary that helped a lot. I sang the songs through for Per before sending them off, sometimes he played along. He turned the contents of our hammock out and got in with his guitar. When he moved his hand, all the long muscles up his arm flexed, the hair stuck out from under his arms. I buried my nose in it and he squeezed me tight.

'Now I've got you.'

'Hm.'

'Come here.'

He drew me in towards him and the guitar fell down with a twang into the heap of dirty washing. We could hardly breathe in that hammock. We lay there looking out. The sunset was different every day, just then it was a big pink stripe over the fields from south to north. We shifted our weight and the hammock started to sway. His mouth was practically inside my ear.

'What should we do?' he whispered. 'I don't know what to do.'

'You mean now?'

'Now, but not just now.'

'Let's wait a bit, then we'll see,' I whispered back. I hadn't thought about it much, I kept avoiding it. I thought about my songs and how I could be of help over in the house, cooking and washing up, hoovering the sofa even if no one would ever notice, polishing the glass tabletop. I thought about the lapwing tumbling over the fallow field at that very moment, pee-wit, pee-wit, its angular wings and little quiff. It was here so early this year, just like every year, the winter was hardly over before the lapwing was back.

17.

It was the twelfth of March, we were lying in the waterbed
and couldn't get up. It was after midday, the sun was shining
and there was a racket coming from the cobbles at the
front. Someone had given Hans-Jakob an old wooden
parlour bench and now he was doing it up. He stood with
a sander in his hand and had been at it for a while. We
were naked under the duvet, looking up at the sloping wall.
There were marks above my head from a foot or a hand.
Then came a sound of laughter, the sander stopped and we
could hear Hans-Jakob talking to someone. Per got halfway
out of bed and leaned over to the window.

'It's my cousin. He's back.'

'The one who was in the States?'

'Yeah, he's down there with my dad.'

'We'd better get up, then.'

'Doesn't matter, he won't mind. Lars!'

He unhasped the window and the sparrows on the

roof flew off as he pushed it open. His cousin shouted back from below, his voice reverberating off the outside walls:

'Hey!'

'When did you get back?'

'Yesterday. The folks came and picked me up.'

'From Cleveland?'

'Ha, ha.'

'Are you coming up? Come on,' said Per and closed the window. He picked his underpants off the floor and pulled them on, hopping about on one foot. I could already hear his cousin on the stairs.

'What about me?' I said and pulled the duvet up under my chin, and then there he was inside the room. They shook hands and hugged. He had longish hair and blue eyes. He had an anorak on and the air around him was cool and fresh, it reached all the way over to me in the bed.

'Bloody hell, I'm out of shape,' he said, and patted his stomach. Per laughed.

'Too many steaks, I bet. You've grown your hair.'

'That makes two of us then,' he said, and turned towards me.

'I'm Lars. You must be Dorte.'

'Yeah, that's Dorte,' said Per.

His handshake was firm. He moved his hand up and down a few times and mine went with it, it made waves in the waterbed. He went over and sat down in the swivel chair, Per searched for some clothes in the hammock.

'Just lying here dossing, the two of you?'

'You could say that,' said Per.

'Have you been out on the town?'

'What town?'

'I was supposed to be going to Pub 22,' I said, pronouncing it all wrong. I cringed but carried on, or it would have made it worse. 'With my aunt. But she couldn't make it in the end.'

'She's got a smørrebrød shop in Ringsted. She's quite young considering,' said Per.

'She'll have had it for twenty years next year,' I said.

'Long time,' said Lars.

'Are you on your bike?' said Per.

'What do you think? Where's your mum?'

'In the house, I suppose.'

'Should we go and see if she's got any coffee?'

'Yeah, let's,' said Per. He'd managed to get his trousers and a T-shirt on now, he came and gave me a kiss.

'We'll go and get some coffee on, then.'

'I'll be over in a bit,' I said.

We all sat round the table in the kitchen. Ruth sat next to Lars and kept putting her hand on his arm or his shoulder.

'He's like a second son to me, can you tell?' she said, and I nodded.

'I can see that.'

'So what are you doing now, until your course starts?' said Hans-Jakob.

'Earning some money at the nursery,' said Lars.

'Have you still got your bedsit in Haslev?'

'Yeah, from April. What about you two?' he said, looking at Per and me. 'Are you going to start studying?'

'At some point,' I said. 'I'm thinking about becoming a teacher.'

'Are you?' said Per.

'Good idea,' said Hans-Jakob.

'I'd think twice if I were you,' said Ruth with a laugh. She patted Lars on the head, he kept looking at me while she was doing it.

'See what I have to put up with?'

He went to the teacher training college in Haslev, his main subjects were biology and physics. I understood he was doing well and got lots of As. It wasn't something he wanted to talk about, he changed the subject. He told us about his younger brother who'd got an apprenticeship in a bakery in Roskilde. He'd made a cake with fourteen tiers and the top one had been decorated with a helicopter made out of boiled sugar. It was for one of his other brothers, the youngest. There were five of them all together, all boys. Lars was the eldest.

'And the second best-looking,' he said with a smile. His blue eyes gleamed across the table.

'Who's number one?' said Ruth.

'Leon, Ruth, as well you know,' said Lars. He pronounced her name the English way and Per laughed.

'Yes, Leon's always had the girls after him.'

'Has he, now?' said Hans-Jakob, turning his teaspoon in the air. He had a wry smile on his face. Ruth had a little dig at him.

'Just like you, in your younger days,' she said and shook her head. Her hair danced on either side of her parting, it was thick and had a good sheen to it. She drank a glass of buttermilk every day and claimed that was why. Lars shook his head too, and smiled.

'Leon's not meant to be on his own.'

'Dorte says that as well,' I said. Lars gave me a puzzled look, Per came to my aid.

'She's the one with the smørrebrød shop. Her aunt.'

'About herself, I mean,' I said, and felt my cheeks going red. Lars reached out for a biscuit from the dish.

'What a lot of Dortes,' he said.

'Don't you want some butter on that?' said Ruth. 'It's good for the brain.'

'Give him a big dollop,' said Hans-Jakob.

He left again after coffee, we all stood on the cobbles and waved goodbye as he got on his racer with the drop handle-bars and took off down the drive. When he got to the road he turned and waved again, Per put both his arms in the air.

'Come back soon,' he shouted, and made his voice crack. He pulled me close, Ruth and Hans-Jakob were already on their way back inside. The parlour bench was in two pieces in the yard, it stayed there for months. I buried my face in the opening of Per's jumper, it smelled a bit musty, an old one from the pile. I could feel him swallowing, ligaments and cartilage bobbing up and down. We stood there like that, and then we went back to ours.

18.

I was named after Dorte because she couldn't have children of her own. They'd given her the diagnosis when she was twenty and already married. It might have been the reason they split up. At any rate, her ex had four kids in no time by a seamstress in Tornemark. They bought a detached that turned out to be built on contaminated land. It cost them a fortune and they were stuck with the place. Dorte's voice grew hollow when she talked about it, she was upset for them regardless. They didn't have a penny to their name, they spent their summer holidays in camping chairs on the patio. Her ex had even done his back in, he fell off a carport. He was nearly fifty now and the only prospect he had left was the knacker's yard, as Dorte put it.

She didn't like talking about that diagnosis. Mostly because it had been so awful the day they told her. She'd cycled all the way to Køge to be examined. The doctor peered between her legs and shook his head.

'Barren,' he said.

She hadn't grasped what he meant. Afterwards she stood for a long time in the waiting room with her coat in her hands, a bomber jacket in blue satin. Eventually she went up and asked the secretary, and the secretary fetched the doctor. He was in the middle of seeing his next patient and came and stood in the doorway with his gynaecologist's headlamp on and his arms at his sides.

'I said you can't have children,' he said, spelling it out, and Dorte stared back at him, she even smiled and thanked him for his time.

That was almost the worst bit. Then when she came out her bike had been stolen, she had to walk nineteen kilometres from Køge to Borup. It was a gorgeous evening in August. There were some young people on tandem bikes in the dwindling light, and couples lying in the wheat fields watching for shooting stars. It was the first time in her life she didn't want to go on living. The bomber jacket was nearly see-through from tears by the time she got home. She stayed in bed for three days, my mum and dad came with cabbage soup. She was small and pale and hugged my mother like a child, burying her face in her apron. But on the fourth day she got up, she had a large brandy and went to the shop for a women's magazine and turned down the corner of every page with nice clothes on it. Not long after that, she got divorced, moved to Roskilde and took her diploma, then lived in Jersie and even Copenhagen, three months in a butcher's shop in Østerbro, before buying the business in Ringsted. It was her anchor all the time she kept moving.

The times I lived with her she always had a laugh sticking a note up next to her name on the door so it said *Dorte Hansen x 2*. Once, the postman rang the bell and asked what it was supposed to mean.

'Exactly what it says,' she told him.

19.

To help me fall asleep I'd started visualising two guards on the bungalow's front step. There had to be two so they could come to each other's aid in an emergency. Sometimes one of them stood by the garden gate, it changed a bit. For weeks I'd been tossing and turning. Whenever I managed to sleep I had nightmares about murders and ferries that sank. Ice drifts, and people who couldn't be trusted. I woke up all sweaty in my pyjamas, fumbling with the buttons under the duvet until eventually I had to sit up to take them off. I put the light on and found a T-shirt in the cupboard, went to the kitchen and drank some water out of a big glass, sat down in the armchair in the front room. I thought about getting a pet of some sort, or at least some curtains. But in the morning, when it got light and the day got started, it never seemed important any more. I sat there knowing I wouldn't buy curtain material the next day either. I'd actually seen some that would have been all right, on the fourth floor of Daells Varehus, some unbleached linen. The girl came up and asked if I needed help. She seemed familiar, a young girl with unusually wide nostrils. She moved some rolls of fabric aside so I could have a better look, then looked at me with a smile.

'Didn't you used to go to school in Næstved?' she said.

'Yes, I did.'

'Me too. You won't remember me, though. I was a year below.'

'Oh, but I thought I recognised you.'

'My hair's different now,' she said, and tossed her head. A strand got stuck in the corner of her mouth, she blew it away. 'Pff. Have you moved here as well?'

'No. I live in Glumsø.'

'Oh, right, just out for the day, then?'

'You could say.'

'I'm reading psychology, as you can see,' she said with a laugh, and I laughed too. I put my hand on the roll and felt the fabric, even though I knew I wasn't going to buy any.

'Is it for curtains?' she said.

'That's what I was thinking. But I think I'll wait a bit.'

'You should get some blinds instead, they're much easier.'

'Maybe I should,' I said, and nodded. I put my hands in my pockets and she moved the top rolls back into place.

'Have a nice day out,' she said.

I waved to her from the stairs, then went up to the cafeteria and had a piece of Othello cake and a cup of coffee, it was nearly twelve so it was lunch of a sort. I was having these cravings for sweets, I think it had to do with being tired. I ate too much rye bread with brown sugar on if I had nothing else in, even at night. It was doing me no good, the energy left me again as quickly as it came.

I sat in the armchair with my legs up underneath me. I'd stopped sweating by then. I decided to stay at home the next day and get a grip on things. Make an omelette for breakfast and squeeze some oranges. Draw up a plan for all the jobs I needed to do. Hoover and go to the library, find some self-help books. They had to have something on sleeping problems. I had a feeling I needed help in other areas as well, but I didn't know which. When I covered my ears with my hands there was a rushing noise inside me that sounded like a whole shoreline. It wasn't worrying in itself. But I had this little flutter under my breastbone, it felt like homesickness. Perhaps it was just acid reflux.

20.

Lars came over a few times a week after his shifts at the nursery. He wore a green anorak and combat trousers, his gardening outfit he called it. His job was transplanting seedlings and potting, thinning out the greenhouses and serving customers. He liked serving customers the best, it made the time go faster. But he enjoyed being outside in the fresh air as well, surrounded by fields with a little seedling between his fingers, and getting paid for it.

We sat on the front step with bottles of beer in our hands. Per had lit a cigarette, he didn't smoke that much any more. Lars coughed and wafted the smoke away. He put his hand on my arm fleetingly when he stopped. I had a woolly jumper on, Ruth had given it me. She'd knitted it for herself years ago, only now it was too tight over her bum. It was blue and white, an Icelandic pattern, and really comfy. Lars got up and stood in front of us with his beer in one hand.

'Who wants to chuck a ball about?'

'Are you sure you're up to it?' said Per.

'You'll have to carry me off if I'm not,' said Lars and laughed. He reached his hand out to Per, Per dropped his cigarette on the ground and crushed it under his trainer, then he took hold and Lars pulled him up. His bottle wobbled on the step, I only just managed to catch it.

The game was up against the wall in what we called the barn. I went with them, over to the sunlounger with the rest of the garden furniture at the far end. It was covered in straw. I brushed it away and sat down. They began whipping the little ball back and forth between the wall and the floor with their bare hands, whacking it hard with their open palms, leaping and lunging. I felt a bit out of place on the lounger, half lying down with my arm over my forehead to protect against any stray balls. They were soon warmed up and sweating. They stopped for a break and pulled off their jumpers, and dumped them at my feet. Per bent down and gave me a quick kiss. He tasted of cigarette.

I began to feel cold. After they'd got started again and played for a while I got up and crossed the yard. My wellies were worn thin, I could feel the cobbles under my feet. The lawn in front of the house was spongy and full of moss. Someone had draped a tennis sock over the boxwood by the patio, I went over and picked it up. I could see

Hans-Jakob on the sofa, lying down reading the paper, he was home early that day. He saw me and smiled. I carried on round the back and through the bushes. At the edge of the garden a pheasant flew up with a cry, it scraped the top of a bare elderberry bush pathetically. I went for a little walk on the bumpy field. When I came back to the garden Lars was standing by the bushes smiling at me with his anorak over his arm.

'Been for a hike?'

'Yes, I was a bit cold. I'm warmer now, though.'

'So now you're taking your clothes off?' he said, and nodded at the tennis sock. I held it up and we looked at it.

'That's right,' I said, and then we laughed.

'That jumper suits you,' he said. 'Did Ruth knit it?'

'Yes, it was hers.'

'Lovely people.'

'I know. I like it here a lot.'

'I don't blame you.'

He put his arm under mine all of a sudden and then we crossed through the garden and out onto the cobbles, Per came towards us in his T-shirt.

'Look, I found a sock,' I said, and waved it about a bit too jauntily.

'Here's your sweetheart,' said Lars to Per, letting go of my arm and giving me a nudge towards him.

'So I see,' said Per.

21.

One day I went for a bike ride while Per was having a nap. I cycled aimlessly in the direction of the nursery, it was late afternoon. The forsythias were in bloom in a few small front gardens. I was soon too hot in my jumper. I stopped to take it off, then carried on in my T-shirt. A smell of seaweed and salt water hung over the fields, they must have been out fertilising. There was a song in my head for a confirmation party. I tried to think of a rhyme for pony, but all I could come up with was stony, phony, bony. The road passed through a little wood, I felt a chill on my arms as I passed through the shade, but then I came out the other side and into the warm air again. I stopped by a solitary tree at the side of the road and folded my jumper tighter on the pannier rack. The sun was very bright. I closed my eyes and turned my face upwards, and stood there for a while. I could hear myself breathing, everything turned red behind my eyelids. The bird we called the bicycle pump chirped somewhere close by, further away I heard the noise of a tractor. I thought: Here I am with only myself. Apart from the sun and the tractor and the bicycle pump. There was a warm breeze against my skin, and my trainers fitted my feet just right, I'd never noticed before. A car approached and I let it go by, my eyes still closed. I wiggled my toes. I stretched my fingers out from the handlebars. By the time I opened my eyes all my thoughts had left me. I got on the bike again and carried slowly on, empty and content. At the nursery I turned down the gravel track, I walked the last bit and leaned the bike against some stacked-up sacks of peat. Lars was in the evergreens behind the goats, I could see his anorak. I looked at the hardy perennials, the grasses and the cactuses, and read all the names. Then I went down to join him, he turned round with a smile, pulled off his glove and gave me his warm, dry hand. He showed me a mahonia shrub, it was a different thing altogether from the tree variety. It was in bloom, with fragrant yellow flowers. We talked for a while. He walked me back to my bike and all the way up the gravel track, where we talked some more.

22.

The library didn't have anything on sleeping problems and I couldn't bring myself to ask if they would order something from another branch. I wandered round the shelves. The librarian was on the phone at her desk, she was having a long and convoluted discussion about storage. She scribbled on a piece of paper with a biro while she spoke. Every now and then she held the pen up in front of her eyes and rolled it between her fingers. Her legs stuck out from under the desk. I recognised the socks, they were the same ones they had in the bookshop window. I found a handbook on literature, only it turned out to be reference only. Instead, I took out a stack of women's magazines and a book of poetry by a girl from Reersø. Then I went out again.

There was a commotion in the street. A lorry from the council had stopped in the middle of the road with its exhaust fuming, it looked like the driver had gone to the chemist's. Behind it was a rubbish truck that couldn't get past, two irate binmen stood in their overalls agreeing with a pedestrian that it wasn't on. The pedestrian's dog had seen something, it was barking madly and straining on the lead. A man in a car blew his horn rhythmically. At the bakery, the assistant stood watching on the step outside. I stopped at the window and looked at the eclairs and the puff pastries with cream.

'Be right with you,' she said, and opened the door for me. I hadn't actually thought of buying anything.

'What a kerfuffle,' she said.

She was about the same age as me. It looked like she might have worked there for quite a while, the way she rearranged the teacakes and brushed away the crumbs. I decided on a pastry snail. As I put the change in my purse the door opened and a stout woman in cropped trousers came in with some difficulty. She leaned over the counter.

'How much are your Linzer tortes?'

'Five fifty.'

'How much are your raspberry slices?'

'Five fifty as well.'

'In that case, I think I'll have a raspberry slice.'

The girl grabbed the one at the front with the tongs and put it in a paper bag. She held the bag open, the woman was still looking.

'How much are your Napoleon hats?'

'Six kroner.'

'Six exactly?'

'Yes.'

'In that case, I think I'll have a Napoleon hat as well.'

'Is it all right in the same bag?'

'Is what all right?'

'The bag. Is it all right in the same bag?'

'I should think so. I don't see why not,' the woman said, and began searching for the right change. I went out with my carrier bag from the library and my pastry snail. The man from the council got into his lorry outside the chemist's, tooted his horn and pulled away with the rubbish truck and the rest of the traffic, a pickup and a pensioner on a moped, following on behind. The procession moved slowly down Østergade. I walked home thinking about the girl at the baker's and what kind of life she had, that and the word kerfuffle. When I came round the corner opposite the station my mum was getting out of the car in front of my house. I turned back quickly towards the pub and stood behind the fence at the back entrance. There was a voice in the kitchen talking about potato salad, the window was wide open. A man came out with an overfilled bin bag. He nodded politely. I walked over to the supermarket car park, then took the short cut round the side of the station. The car was still outside the house, but my mum was nowhere to be seen. I stood behind a tree for a bit, then scurried round the back of the station all the way to the end of the platform. I stepped behind the bushes. It was half past one. The trees on the other side had turned yellow and red, every little gust of wind sent leaves fluttering onto the tracks. I waited a quarter of an hour before going back. The car was gone by then. My mum had pushed a note through the letter box and left a pack of coffee in the shed.

I couldn't enjoy that pastry snail. I sat in bed and nibbled at it while flicking through the magazines from the library. One of them had an article about lethargy entitled 'SLUGS AND SNAILS'. I tried to remember the rest of the rhyme but couldn't, all I could think about was the coincidence of snails. I made coffee out of my mum's coffee. I'd run out of milk so I had to sweeten it more than usual.

In the evening I hung a big bath towel and a sheet up in front of the windows in the front room and tried on all my clothes. I carried the mirror in from the hall. I painted my nails and decided I needed a new look and a new way of thinking and walking. I even thought I might put a piece together for a newspaper, I just didn't know what about. There was nothing in particular I was good at, except perhaps writing lyrics for party songs, but I didn't even do that any more. Instead, I wrote a list of things I ought to see and do in Copenhagen. I was full of good ideas. For once, I fell asleep straight away, but then woke up again far too early. The front room looked like an explosion in a second-hand shop, and I'd got nail varnish on the lamp. I tidied up and got dressed. I was ready before six. I caught the five-past-nine.

23.

Instead of going on to Copenhagen I got off at Ringsted and walked up to the smørrebrød shop. Dorte was standing on the step round the back having a fag. A smell of roast meat was coming from inside. She threw out her arms when she saw me.

'Hello, love, what a nice surprise. What brings you here?'

She gave me a hug, holding the cigarette at arm's length, and kissed me on the cheek.

'We haven't got lectures today,' I said.

'How come?'

'We just don't have them every day.'

'Well then, come in. It's lovely to see you. Are you in the dumps?'

'Not really.'

'Yes, you are. I can tell.'

'No, I'm just tired, that's all.'

'I can see that. Your eyes are all wrong.'

'I'm not sleeping very well.'

'Is it the trains?'

'No, I quite like the trains.'

'You like the house all right, don't you?'

'Yes, I do.'

'Well, you look gorgeous no matter how tired you are,' she said and kissed me again, then we went into the kitchen, she got a cup out for me and poured me a coffee from the Thermos on the table.

'Do you fancy a cheese sandwich?' she said.

'No, thanks.'

'Are you slimming?'

'Sort of.'

'What do you think of this, by the way?' she said, extending her fingers towards me. Her nails were coral-coloured, they looked nice against her hands.

'It looks nice against your hands,' I said.

'Yes, I think so too. That's nice, though,' she said, indicating my own fingers with their short, plum-coloured nails.

'I've got fat fingers,' I said, and fluttered them about.

'You have *not*.'

'I have *too*.'

'Your hair suits you when you put it up like that,' she said.

'Above the ears, you mean?'

'A bit piled up, with stray strands. I like that. How come you aren't sleeping?'

I shrugged.

'I don't know.'

'Can you keep up with your studies?'

'Mm.'

'Do you like the course? Are you getting on all right with it?'

'Yes, fine.'

'Fine means not fine at all.'

'No, it doesn't. Fine's fine,' I said and gulped a mouthful of coffee. She did likewise, then wiped the outline of her lipstick with her finger.

'Well, I'm pleased.'

'Mm.'

'Do you remember the time I lay awake in Lübeck?' she said. I remembered it well and nodded. She'd been on a coach trip with a new man. He was tall and ruddy, she fitted under his arm when they walked along the street. She'd never had one as tall as him before, but fortunately he had a paunch as well. I can't be doing with a man with no belly, she always said. The coach left from in front of the train station in Næstved, it turned out she knew some of the people who were going. They all stood with their luggage, chattering in the early-morning light. She had her cobalt-blue trouser suit on and a scarf that billowed nicely about her neck in the wind. They all seemed so happy and excited. Every time she said hello to someone new, her laughter increased. She threw her hands in the air and laughed and laughed at her own excitement. They'd booked a room with a balcony, she thought they might sit out with a bottle of prosecco and some Twiglets. She got the window seat on the coach, there was a little carton of juice in the pocket in front of every seat, she could hardly sit still.

'Oh, look at this! There's juice,' she said. And then shortly afterwards:

'Look at the roundabout there! Look at that girl!'

And the next moment as they left the town:

'Look at all those birds. I've never seen so many!'

'They're called seagulls,' said the woman in the seat behind, and some people began to laugh. Dorte laughed even louder then and twisted round in her seat half standing up. She put her hand on top of the woman's on the headrest.

'Are they really seagulls? I think I'm dyslexic with birds.'

After she sat down again and had been quiet for a second with a smile still on her face, her boyfriend leaned over and said:

'I think you should settle down now, don't you?'

It was as if all the life drained away from her. She couldn't say how it happened. The corners of her mouth drooped. Her arms went limp. She turned her head away and looked out at the fresh green fields and trees and the roe deer as they ran. Nothing had ever seemed so sad to her. And they hadn't even got as far as Mogenstrup. Her hands lay dead in her lap on top of her cobalt-blue trousers. She thought: I'm nothing but an empty frame. After Bårse, her boyfriend looked at her with a smile.

'Aren't you going to have your juice, Dorte?'

She couldn't answer. All she could do was shake her head, the slightest of movements.

'Eh?'

'I can't,' she whispered, and turned very slowly away, stared out at the blue sky, the white trails left by the planes, the life that wasn't going to be hers after all, woods all to no use. On the ferry crossing from Rødby to Puttgarden she cheered up briefly when she bought a lipstick and the girl in the shop complimented her on her choice.

'Such a lovely colour, that.'

'Yes, it's nice,' she managed to say with a little smile.

But the three days they were in Lübeck she hardly said a word. She poked at her schnitzels, and raised her glass without drinking whenever anyone said cheers. Both nights she lay stretched out on her back with her eyes wide open, it was like they wouldn't close. She hadn't a thought in her head, only emptiness. She didn't fall asleep until they were on the bus home, they were on the outskirts of Oldenburg and it was only for fifteen minutes, but when she woke up she wanted a cup of coffee. A big one, and black. Preferably her own at home, followed by a good film and a foot bath. All by herself in her own cosy flat, and as soon as she found time she was going to change all the furniture around. When the thought came to her that the sofa would go better by the window, she realised she was starting to perk up again.

I stayed in the shop for a couple of hours and helped her carve the roast and do the salad and oranges. She was trying out a new special as well, a kind of pastrami roll, I arranged fifteen of them on a tray. The rest she'd make as she went along. She stepped out the back with me when it was time for me to go. We stood chatting for a bit while she had a smoke, and then we gave each other a hug. She coughed over my shoulder.

'Oh, I nearly forgot,' she said. 'Are you slimming too much for some roast?'

'I don't suppose I am,' I said, and she wrapped a piece of meat in greaseproof and put it in a carrier bag for me, along with two oranges, a packet of rye bread and three hundred kroner. I gave her a kiss on the cheek.

'I haven't even asked how you're getting on with Hardy,' I said.

'Oh, fine,' she said. So she wasn't.

'I'm glad,' I said.

24.

One day when I was browsing on Larsbjørnsstræde one of the assistants from the big vintage shop was standing on the corner crying. It was the girl with the white hair and the shoes. She turned aside as I went by, but I could still hear her sobbing even though she tried to control herself. I crossed over to the other side and went into Janus. I'd seen some Mexican drinking glasses upstairs, but on closer inspection I wasn't keen. I looked out of the window and could see she was still there. One of the other assistants came out and stood with her for a bit. Then they went back inside together. I tried on a baggy jumper and ended up buying it. It would go with a pair of leggings once I started wearing leggings. I'd been to that vintage shop lots of times, you could hardly cross the floor for lace-up boots, and their clothes were all jammed together on the racks: men's shirts and suit jackets, and discarded pyjamas. Every time you pulled an item out, two others came with it. There was a sour, dusty smell about the place, which I liked. I bought a pair of leg warmers there once and wore them on my arms in the evenings in the front room when I was cold. The two assistants stood flicking through a notebook at the counter when I came in. I rummaged through a bin of underskirts while I waited for them to say something. I found a light blue one with white trim. Eventually, the one who'd been crying said:

'But there were *four* of them.'

'I know, that's what *I* said,' said the other. They looked down at me as I pulled the underskirt out. I looked at the size and examined the trim, then put it back.

'It can't ever have been five,' said the one who'd been crying.

'No, you'd be dead otherwise, wouldn't you?'

I carried on browsing through the racks and bins, but unfortunately they didn't say anything more after that. I could feel them looking at me. After a while I decided on a pair of woollen gloves and put them down on the counter. The one who'd been crying entered the amount into the till. I handed her a twenty-krone note and she said:

'You do Danish, don't you?'

'Not me,' I said.

'Oh, I thought I'd seen you on the Amager campus.'

'I thought so too,' said the other one from behind a pile of shirts.

'I recognised you from your cheeks.'

'Sorry,' I said, and put the gloves in my bag. 'It must have been someone else. Bye.'

'Bye, then,' they said.

I went down the stairs and out into the street. I walked back towards the Strøget, then went into a shop on the corner, through the shoes and upstairs to the women's department. I took a random tweed coat off the peg and went into a fitting room. I looked at my face from all sides in the two mirrors, smiling and not smiling. After that I tried the coat on, it didn't look bad at all. But then on the train home I decided to give it to Dorte. I'd never wear it anyway. I once heard her speak highly of tweed on a trip to Gisselfeld, a rare Sunday outing with my mum and dad to look at the old oak trees. We had coffee in a lay-by on the way back.

When I got off the train, the guy from the ticket office was sitting on the bench by the platform. The office was closed now, he was listening to his Walkman.

'Finished for the day?' I said as I went past. He was in his shirtsleeves, he took off his headphones and smiled.

'Sorry?'

'I said I see you've finished for the day.'

'Oh, right. Actually, I've locked myself out,' he said.

'You haven't? But you're closed now, aren't you?'

'Yeah. I meant the flat.'

He jerked his head and pointed up at the first floor at the same time.

'My keys are inside. My girlfriend's off now though, I'm just waiting till she gets in.'

'On the train?'

'Yeah, she works in Vordingborg.'

'So you're the ones who live upstairs?'

He nodded.

'Yeah.'

'Oh, I see now. You haven't got far to work, then. Aren't you cold like that?'

'It's not too bad.'

'You can wait at mine if you want, I only live over there,' I said, and pointed in the direction of the house. He nodded.

'I know. It's okay, she'll be here soon.'

'All right. See you, then,' I said, and pulled the handle of the waiting-room door. It was locked, I wasn't thinking. I shook my head at myself and smiled at him.

'School for the gifted,' I said in English. He nodded and looked a bit puzzled.

When I got round the corner I remembered the coat. I went back and took it out of the bag.

'You can borrow this while you're waiting,' I said.

We sat on the bench together, with him in the tweed. He lent me the headphones and I listened to one of his favourite tracks. I listened without saying anything, now and then he gave me a nod and raised his eyebrows, and I nodded back. His hands were small and rather broad. The sleeves of the coat stopped short of his wrists. When the train appeared from between the trees he stood up. We were still joined by the Walkman, so I had to stand up with him. I removed the headphones and handed them back, he took off the coat and did likewise.

'Thanks for your help. See you, then,' he said.

'Yeah, see you,' I said and remained standing by the bench as the train pulled in. I turned, then folded the coat and put it carefully back in the bag. She came up to him, I could hear them behind my back.

'Hi.'

'Hi, what are you doing here?'

'I locked myself out.'

'It's a good thing I'm early, then.'

'You did say *four*.'

'It could just as well have been five.'

'I'd be dead by then,' he said with a laugh, and I looked up and saw them disappear round the corner. Just as I thought, it was the girl who'd come over that night the picnic couple had stayed, but that didn't matter now. I stood there with my coat in the bag and the coincidence of four, five, dead. It didn't mean a thing, but still it was so weird I couldn't get my head round it. I once saw a programme about a woman who saw signs everywhere, she did her shopping and her workouts and slept according to what she saw. Eventually she got divorced when everything else around her started coming apart as well, chairs and tools and stitching in particular. The stitching wasn't relevant in itself, but like she said: a person sees and hears only what they want to. I walked home with my coat. I let myself in and made some coffee. The same programme had a bit on a little Austrian man who'd had the hiccups for twenty-eight years. I'd seen him in the papers, but all of a sudden there he was hiccuping away while he talked about his condition. He could have talked about anything at all, really. It might have been better if he'd talked about something else entirely.

25.

It rained. The parlour bench disintegrated on the cobbles. Hans-Jakob experimented with baking bread in the afternoons, trying out methods of raising and different kinds of flour. He did a very successful loaf in a pot and served it oozing with butter. Ruth asked to have her mouth taped shut after six slices. Hans-Jakob got the first-aid tin out of the Volvo and snipped off a length of sticking plaster. He ran round the whole downstairs after her, she shrieked and squealed. I'd been at work that day, Ruth had insisted on giving me a lift even though she had no lessons because of exams. On the way, she picked up two hitch-hikers. One of them had dreadlocks. They spoke fractured German and were on their way to Sweden. They sat in the back and kept thanking us, they even gave us a bag of liquorice allsorts and a miniature bottle of cognac. Ruth dropped them off at the ring road and did the shopping while I helped Niller with his homework. After I was finished I waited for her under the roof of the bike sheds. She smiled and waved behind the steamed-up windscreen when she saw me, then leaned across the seat and opened the door.

'Come in out of the rain. How was it?'

'It was fine.'

'It smells like a henhouse in here,' she said. 'But they were very sweet.'

'I think it was really nice of you to give them a lift,' I said. 'A lot of people wouldn't.'

'They'd be kind in other ways instead. Do you want an allsort?'

'Yes please.'

'Is there anything you want while we're out? Anything you need?'

'No, not really.'

'I got you this, by the way,' she said, reaching for a carrier bag on the back seat. It was a book we'd read about in the paper, short stories about the future written by young people from the Storstrøm region. It had been reviewed under the headline 'CARDBOARD AND CACK'. We drove a different way home. Ruth had heard about a place that sold honey from a stall in Alsted. We drove round and round but couldn't find it. When we pulled out onto the main road again she asked if I wanted to stop by my mum and dad's to say hello, but I didn't.

'I'd like to thank them, if I could,' she said.

'What for?'

'What do you think what for?' she said and smiled at me. I smiled back and offered her an allsort from the bag. She took two or three and drove with one hand on the wheel.

Just as Hans-Jakob caught up with her with his plaster, Ruth managed to open the patio door and ran outside into the rain in her socks. He stopped for a moment and swore, then ran out after her. We watched them from inside the house. They jigged over the cobbles, then he caught her by the barn. She squealed again. At the same moment, Lars came cycling up the drive in his waterproofs. It had been a while since we'd seen him last. He got off and wheeled the bike over and leaned it up against the wall. We could see them laughing together. Then they came back up to the house, Ruth's hair was a wet curtain now, and their socks left puddles on the floor. Lars took his waterproofs off and dumped them in the utility room. We all stood and chatted for a bit in the kitchen, and then Ruth and Hans-Jakob said they were going to have a bath. They disappeared upstairs, we heard their footsteps above our heads, then a bit later the faint rush of water in the pipes. Per went to get a new LP he'd bought so we could listen to it on the stereo. We watched him from the kitchen window as he crossed over the cobbles in his wellies.

We went into the living room while he was gone. We looked out at the garden and the woods beyond the beech hedge. Their green was so pale it was nearly yellow. He put his hand on my shoulder, I turned towards him and then we kissed. Per came back with his LP. We sat on the sofa and listened to it a couple of times. The fire was burning in the stove. When Per went to the bathroom we kissed again. We had osso bucco for dinner, we laughed and talked and drank red wine, and I didn't have a decent thought in my head, everything was pulling at me. We sat at the table until way past midnight. Lars stayed over and slept on the sofa, and I lay awake most of the night in the bedsit next to Per. His breath was heavy and warm. Around three I opened the window and heard a nightingale somewhere in the drizzle. It was all too much. I would never be able to share it with anyone, ever. Per stirred and whispered my name. I closed the window quietly and got back into bed.

26.

In the evenings I could see the guy from the ticket office in the upstairs flat with his girlfriend, walking about in what must have been the living room. His girlfriend was often in the kitchen. Every now and then she'd open the window and shake out a tea towel. I thought about what reasons there might be to shake out a tea towel. Sometimes he sat smoking at the living-room window. He sat with his chin in his hand, puffing little clouds of smoke out in front of his pale face. They had a big cowboy cactus, in one of the other windows. One night I had a letter to post, I was humming to myself as I walked over to the postbox with it. It was an application for a student loan. When I was almost right underneath him, he cleared his throat and I glanced about, startled, before saying hello.

'Are you keeping warm all right?' he said from above.

'Just about.'

'It's starting to get cold now,' he said, and took a drag on his cigarette. His cheeks hollowed in the dim light.

'My central heating's oil-fired,' I said.

'Yeah?'

'What about you, is yours from the network?'

'No, we're on oil too. The boiler's down there. It heats the whole place up,' he said, and twirled a finger in the air.

I nodded. He nodded too.

'It must be a big boiler, then,' I said.

'I suppose so,' he said. 'I wouldn't know to be honest. It looks fairly normal to me.'

We both laughed. He stubbed his cigarette out on the window ledge and flicked it outside into the air. It landed under the lamp post, and then the toilet flushed. The bathroom door must have been opened at the same time, the sound was that clear. He smiled down at me.

'See you around, then.'

'Yeah, see you.'

I was going to have meatloaf, but when I stood in the kitchen with the minced meat and the box of eggs I decided I couldn't be bothered. I boiled the mince and had it in a pitta bread with a bit of cucumber. I'd stopped eating at the table, I couldn't enjoy my food sitting in front of the window. I put a removal box next to the armchair and used that as a table instead, I practised eating my food slowly, it was quite hard to do on your own. Dorte had a method she used when her clothes started feeling tight, she lit a cigarette and took a drag between mouthfuls. Besides that she could say no to almost everything. The best way to lose weight was to shake your head, she said.

It had turned really cold now. The floor was draughty and I traipsed about in my boots indoors. Sometimes the boiler went out and I had to fill it up with water, there was a special length of hose for the purpose. I'd filled it up quite a few times already. After a week the pressure dropped and the needle was in the red again. I didn't know where it all went. When the boiler was going it was nice and hot in the utility room. I started drying my clothes in there, I'd hammered a couple of nails in the wall and put a clothes line up. Once, I sat and had my dinner there. I'd been sitting still so long in the front room I was frozen stiff. Afterwards I ran a bath and got in, but I couldn't relax, I kept hearing something scratching as I lay there looking up at the ceiling. A bit of straw stuck out from a crack.

I went to bed conscientiously before midnight. I tossed and turned and kept deciding to get some exercise the next day. I counted backwards from increasingly high numbers. It did everything but send me to sleep. I'd put too much garlic in the mince, it had given me a stomach ache. I got annoyed with myself about everything: too much garlic and not enough money, my stupid prattling on about boilers to the guy from the ticket office. I got up again and stepped into my boots, put my dressing gown on over my T-shirt and went out into the front garden. I gave the apple tree a good kicking. It didn't help, all it did was leave me out of breath. I stood there getting it back. The light from the street lamp slanted across the lawn. Then I heard a faint cough from over by the station, the ticket-office guy was having a smoke on the step. He was in his dressing gown too, a white one. Mine was pink. I didn't think he'd seen me in the dark, but then he stepped down and came over.

27.

I once asked Dorte if she felt just as besotted every time she found someone new. She gave a shrug.

'Pretty much.'

'What goes wrong then?'

'I'm not sure anything actually goes wrong. Sometimes I'd rather be on my own all of a sudden. You know how awkward I can be.'

'But do you get sick of them?'

'I don't know, it's hard to explain really. Anyway, it's not always me who ditches them. Take Henning, for instance,' she said, and shook her head. We were sitting at her table with a sponge cake, it was raining. It might have been a bank holiday, at any rate she wasn't going in to the shop. We'd had a long chat about her upstairs neighbours who had unexpectedly split up. Dorte was quite taken aback. She'd seen them holding hands at the cold counter only a few weeks before, they'd been looking at the salami.

'What do you think?' one of them said.

'I don't know. What do you think?' said the other.

She may well have felt like giving them both a kick up the arse, as she put it, but at the same time she couldn't help feeling a bit envious. She thought: How come they can make a go of it when I can't? Every time she found someone, she thought he was the one. Only then he'd turn out to have an annoying habit of droning on or putting jam on top of his cheese, or collecting bottles whenever they were out walking in the park so he could claim the deposit. Henning had done that. She couldn't understand why he kept lagging behind. He even had a rucksack to put them in, but from the start she'd decided not to interfere. He was a journalist on the local paper, he read novels and biographies. He insisted on going home and sleeping in his own bed at night. She only went to his flat once, it was dark and untidy, but she didn't interfere in that either. She gave him a key to her own place and wiped newspaper smudges off the door frames when he wasn't there. After a few weeks she found herself pestering him to stay the night, it was a Saturday. He grumbled a bit at first, but after a while he gave in.

She kept waking up that night and smiling at him in the dark. She lay and watched the clock turn seven and eight before getting up. She crept out to the bathroom and got herself ready. At nine she put the coffee on. At half nine she made the toast. At ten she made some more, but it was half ten by the time she heard him stir. She sat up in her chair and forced a smile.

'Sleepyhead,' she said when he came in.

'Mm,' he said and touched her shoulder. He sat down and took a piece of toast.

'I've had mine,' she said. 'I couldn't wait any longer. I waited ages. I always look forward to breakfast.'

He pulled a little corner off and put it in his mouth. She thought: I need to be broad-minded now.

'I imagined we'd have breakfast together,' she said.

And then a moment later:

'A grown man lying in until half past ten.'

He paused for a second in the middle of his toast, then carried on munching. He had another cup of coffee and went to the bathroom. She sat looking out of the window at the traffic below, a pedestrian saw her and waved. She didn't wave back. A good bit later he came in again, he had his coat and rucksack on. He lifted a couple of fingers by way of goodbye.

'Cheers for now, then,' he said.

Her lips were so tight she couldn't get a word out. She sat, rigid, at the table for nearly an hour. Eventually she got the better of herself and went over to his, but there was no answer. She found a crumpled piece of paper in her bag and wrote: *Did you go because you were going, or have you gone?* She folded it up and put it through the letter box. She'd seen him once since, on his way in to the Kvickly supermarket. He saw her too. They both turned away. Annoyingly, he was quicker.

Anyway, her upstairs neighbours hadn't been able to make a go of it either, and they'd been together more than eight years. Dorte could hear the woman crying at night. She'd bumped into her on the stairs too. She looked like she'd been steeped in chlorine.

'It's funny,' she said, 'because I can see she's having a hard time of it. I just don't understand how it can hurt that much. I mean, she's still young. Her future's wide open.'

'She must miss him,' I said.

'Yes, but still.'

'Perhaps it's like if you were never going to see me again,' I said.

'Do you think? I can't imagine that at all. What a terrible thought.'

'That's probably what it's like then.'

'Oh, that's awful. Do you know, I might just pop in on her with a little bunch of something once I've got a minute,' she said.

28.

Per and Ruth and Hans-Jakob invited me with them to
Sweden for the Whitsun holiday, three days at a hotel by
a lake in Småland. We drove up in the Volvo, Per and me
in the back with a pillow each. We held hands across the
seat, Per rubbed my palm with his thumb. I took my hand
away and propped the pillow up between my cheek and
the window and stared out at the vast pine forests. Ruth
did the driving, Hans-Jakob sat with the map and a bar of
Marabou chocolate. He broke pieces off and handed them
back to us. They'd booked us into two rooms. There was
a dinner included, in a banqueting room. We were going
to have coffee in a summer house in the garden then go
down to the freezing cold lake for an evening swim. Per
had his checked shorts on, his thighs were long and firm.
He took hold of my hand again, then leaned across and
put his lips to my ear.

'Are you tired, darling?'

'A bit.'

'You're not carsick, are you?'

'No.'

'How about stopping at the next lay-by?' he said to Ruth, and she nodded.

'Good idea. I'll have a piece of that too, Hans-Jakob.'

We ambled back and forth in the lay-by. Per swung our arms. He shoved me into a little ditch and pulled me up again. Ruth and Hans-Jakob sat on the bench and studied the map. Hans-Jakob waved to us.

'Look at him, the old fart,' said Per.

'Don't talk about your dad like that,' I said.

'He's eaten nearly all that chocolate himself now.'

'He's only forty-five. He can still thrash you at badminton.'

'Ha, ha.'

'Ow, that hurts.'

'I'd like to get old with you someday,' he said.

'No, you wouldn't.'

'What do you mean? Yes, I would.'

'You don't want to get old.'

'No, but the other bit.'

'That's nice of you to say,' I said. He put his arms around

me from behind and kissed me on the neck, and nudged me on towards his parents. Ruth looked up.

'Still kissing after four hundred kilometres,' she said.

In the evening we lay naked in our room after the swim, our bellies full of elk steaks and French red wine. Our bathing costumes were hanging up to dry on the balcony. A piano played downstairs, and on the other side of the wall behind our bed I could hear Ruth's voice. There was a scraping sound, perhaps from a piece of furniture, followed by chinking glasses and laughter. When I turned to Per he'd fallen asleep. I began to cry, ever so quietly at first, but then I let go. I sniffed and sobbed. Eventually, he woke and sat up.

'What's wrong?' he said. 'Have you had too much wine?'

'No.'

'What's the matter then? Is it something I've done?'

'No.'

'What then?'

'It's just that you'd fallen asleep. I felt so alone all of a sudden.'

'Come here,' he said, and drew me towards him. I cried all down his smooth shoulder.

'I can't bear the thought that we're so young, either. We're much too young.'

'For what?'

'For everything. For this. We're just waiting for it to fall apart.'

'What kind of a thing's that to say in the middle of the night, you bloody great arse?' he said, and then he began to cry as well, the tears streamed down his cheeks. He picked up the pillow and buried his face in it. I didn't know what to do. He curled up and made some long, hollow sounds. After a bit I leaned forward and took the pillow away. His hair stuck to his forehead.

'I'm sorry. I didn't mean it like that,' I said.

'Is that why you've been acting so strange?' he said.

'No. I'm sorry,' I said.

'What are you trying to tell me then?'

'That was it. I just thought we were so young all of a sudden.'

'What am I supposed to say to that? There's nothing I can say,' he said. There was an unfamiliar anger in his voice that I liked.

'I know,' I said.

'It's up to you what you want,' he said. 'It's got nothing to do with being young or not.'

But the next morning his anger had evaporated, he kept touching me fondly as we ate our cinnamon rolls. Ruth was playing around with a box of matches. Her coffee spilled over onto the white tablecloth. Every time I looked out I thought about my suitcase. It was drizzling and the grass was all green. I imagined sitting on a bus with my hands in my lap, then getting off. I thought about the suitcase when the others were busy and when I was on my own, as I stood by the window in the room that looked out on the lake and when I lay there in bed. After we got home it seemed like the only thing to do was pack. I did it on the Tuesday morning before Per woke up, and when he did I told him. I carried the suitcase down the stairs and put it down under the sycamore tree while I got my bike out of the barn. Per stood on the cobbles in his underpants. When I went up to kiss him he turned away. I put the suitcase on the pannier rack and wheeled the bike down the drive. When I got to the road I turned round. He was still standing there. He didn't move. I thought about raising my hand, and then I did.

29.

It was a bit of a job wheeling the bike with the suitcase on the pannier rack, it kept sliding to one side. Every now and then I had to stop and manoeuvre it back into place, there was hardly any strength left in my arms after a couple of kilometres. Just before Teestrup a white van slowed down, inside were two men wearing overalls. One of them rolled the window down.

'Do you need any help?'

'No, thanks.'

'It'll go in the back no bother.'

'No, I'm all right, thanks.'

'Where are you going? Are you going to Ringsted?'

'No, just over there,' I said, and pointed. They both turned their heads and looked. I moved my finger a bit to the right, towards a building on the other side of a wire fence.

'Well, give them our love,' he said, and then they drove on. The other one smirked in the mirror.

The building was a disused electricity substation. The van was long gone, but I stopped by the fence anyway and put the suitcase on the ground. I sat down on it. It gave a bit, ominously, underneath me, I shifted my weight further forward onto my legs. I was wearing trainers, the laces slapped against them. I was terribly thirsty. I'd packed a carton of apple juice but I couldn't be bothered to unearth it. Now and then a car went past. Then a bit later a fat woman on a moped. She got a fright when she saw me. I sat and listened as the sound of the vehicle grew fainter, then I got my juice out. The sun was beating down, my arms were shaking from my struggle with the suitcase. After a bit the sound came back from somewhere far off to the right. It got louder, and eventually the woman from before rolled up in front of me. She switched off the engine and took off her helmet.

'Everything all right?'

'Yes,' I said and took a sip of my juice. The straw gurgled. She had a denim skirt on and a waistcoat with tassels, she stood straddling the moped.

'I just thought all of a sudden you looked a bit forlorn. I'd nearly got to Haslev,' she said.

'Oh,' I said.

'Glad to hear you're all right, though.'

'Yes, I'm fine. Thanks.'

'Then I began to wonder if you might be going into town as well. I thought if you were, I could give you a pull.'

'But there's this,' I said, and pointed down at the suitcase.

'True,' she said. 'But we could pick that up after. How far have you come with it?'

'I don't know. Five kilometres, maybe.'

'Ouch.'

'So I don't think I could hold on for a pull just at the minute. It's really kind of you, all the same,' I said.

She nodded.

'Tell you what, then. We'll leave the bike instead. You have your drink, there's no rush,' she said. So I finished my juice and got to my feet, squeezed the air out of the carton and stuffed it in the waist of my trousers for want of anywhere better. She put her helmet on again. Then she picked up my suitcase and wedged it diagonally between her legs. It looked precarious. She started the moped and jerked her thumb towards the pannier rack. I got on and we wobbled off.

We crawled along. I put my arms around her waist. Her waistcoat smelled of something familiar, sun cream or melon. I thought it must be hard for her to steer. Her thighs and calves clamped the suitcase tight, but she could still nod her head to the left when we passed by a hare in a meadow. It pricked up its ears.

I'd had a vision of Haslev. But as soon as we entered the town I forgot what it was. The roads were wide and dusty, manhole covers clonked under our wheels. We pulled up on a little square with empty hanging baskets, they looked like ones we'd had at home. I got off, and she extracted herself.

'Are you all right from here? You sure you don't need somewhere to stay?' she said through her visor.

'No, I'm fine, really. Thanks for the lift.'

'Thanks for the company. Do you want me to pick up your bike at some point?'

'No need. I'll just walk back and get it.'

'Right you are. I'll be off to the baker's, then. Look after yourself,' she said, and held out her hand. It was soft and moist.

I stood and watched as she pulled away. She turned and waved before disappearing round a corner by some redbrick flats. I laid the suitcase down and opened it and got my money out. Then I stood it on its end again and draped a top over it. I left it where it was and crossed the road to a corner shop where I bought three small cartons of juice and a packet of biscuits. When I came out Lars was standing on the square with a vanload of hanging fuchsias. For a second I thought it was some kind of welcome. It was such an odd coincidence all we could do was act normal. I gave him a juice and hid the biscuits away in my suitcase.

30.

I lived with Lars in his bedsit in Haslev. We had a daybed with storage, and a corner unit and a desk that doubled as a dinner table. Every morning after he'd gone I went down into the little courtyard and picked a handful of flowers and arranged them in the pewter mug on the desk. I washed my hair in egg yolk, I walked round the town looking at clothes and jewellery. I bought coconut milk and packet noodles, and a funny purple fruit we couldn't get open. The kitchen and bathroom were communal. The guy next door was from Egøje, he never rinsed the sink after himself. One of the others was a driving instructor. Lars was going back to teacher training college after the summer holiday, he was so tanned his stubble was luminous. He lay on the daybed with his hands behind his head, while I sat at the table looking at him. Or else I'd read a newspaper he'd brought home from the nursery and fiddle with the arrangement in the mug. We ate lots of potatoes with cold gravy.

When we hugged, my eyes would blink madly behind his shoulder.

We didn't go round the town together, we never went anywhere at all. I practised walking with a straight back, up and down Jernbanegade in a new yellow dress. I'd bought a pair of strappy high heels too. In the evenings I set the table nicely and we'd eat with the door of the French balcony open. There were two little girls who often played in the yard. They made dens behind a bush and had doll's tea parties. I stood at the balcony door and waved to them, sometimes they waved back. I called for Lars to come and see, but they didn't interest him much. I polished my nails with cotton wool dipped in sunflower oil. Now and then we had wine with our meal, diluted with sparkling water. I had a very small appetite, so I began to eat butter. I never had breakfast until after he'd gone. I made myself a piece of toast and a cup of coffee. I sat with a crossword while I drank the coffee. Afterwards I did a bit of dusting and let some air in. I washed the bed sheets in the laundry room in the basement. As soon as the washing machine had started I hurried back upstairs and set the egg timer. I lay down gently on the daybed so as not to mess up my hair, I'd started putting it up with hairpins. I tried to read but couldn't concentrate. I couldn't picture what I read. Lars read Kafka, he didn't see the point in reading anything else. When he read, his eyes darted from side to side. I wondered if mine did the same thing and if it was flattering. I plucked my eyebrows in a hand mirror in front of the balcony door. I took my clothes off even before he got home, and stood in various poses by the desk. I had my photo taken with a bowler hat on. The hat was kept on the corner unit, balanced on a bottle of Bacardi.

Once in a while I went and phoned Per. The nearest phone box was by the cinema. I always made sure to have five-krone coins with me, but I never needed them. His voice was by turns exuberant and weary. I asked how he was feeling and he said they were going to Anholt for the holidays. Then after that to Bulgaria. Only he didn't know if he wanted to go to Bulgaria. It'd be nice to have the place to himself without the folks around, he said, and then he started crying. There was a rustling noise as he drew away. I stood there breathing into the black receiver, it steamed up. Then Ruth came on the line.

'Listen, please don't ring Per up any more. He gets far too upset,' she said.

'I'm sorry,' I said.

'So please don't.'

'I'm very sorry,' I said. My palm was moist from clutching my change. I went the long way home. It was a Tuesday, market day on the square. I bought a carton of strawberries and a peach, and ate the peach as I walked.

It dripped on my yellow dress. I prepared the strawberries and put them in the fridge. After that I lay down on the floor in front of the open balcony door and sunbathed. I used the sunbeds just past the church too, they cost ten kroner for twenty-five minutes. Two girls took turns on reception, one of them had thick hair and eyes like a cat. She spoke with a Jutland accent, I wondered what she was doing in Haslev.

'Do you want to book another session while you're here?'

'Yes, please. For tomorrow.'

'Are you on holiday?'

'You could say.'

'Brilliant,' she said, and put me in the book for three o'clock.

'Yes, brilliant,' I said, I'd be able to get home and have a bath before Lars got off work. I found myself thinking she was probably his type, she had nice, neat hands. I washed the peach stain off under the tap, it dried again in a jiffy. My hair was almost white from the sun, it suited me. I put the dress back on and set the table with glasses and cutlery. Then I thought better of it and put it all back in the unit. I was sitting with *The Castle* in front of me when he came home. First he had a rest and after that a bath. Then he stood for a bit and looked out of the window without saying anything.

'There's strawberries, I nearly forgot,' I said, and went out to the kitchen, only they were gone. It was the guy from Egøje.

At night we lay snuggled up close. The wind rushed in the treetops behind the building. When one of us couldn't sleep we'd wake the other one up, it was an agreement we had. After that we usually fell asleep. The alarm went off at half seven, he was on eight till four. One Friday he said he'd be late home. It was one of his brothers' eighteenth birthday and there was going to be cake and spit-roasted suckling pig at his mum and dad's. I stood in the kitchen and waved to him when he left. I did the same every morning. He had green shorts and a T-shirt on. He turned and waved again at the top of the road. Now I had a whole day and an evening to while away. I let some air in and tidied the place up in no time. I sat and picked raisins out of the muesli. I counted my money. I needed to get some more out. Shortly before half past nine I went down to the bank. I bought an enormous ice cream from the sweet shop. I was the first customer of the day. I sat on the little square with the hanging baskets and ate it. Afterwards, I felt so drowsy I had to go home and have a lie-down. When I woke up I had a bath and cleaned the sink. It was just gone eleven by then. I tidied my clothes and put them away in neat piles. I squeezed a lemon and put the juice in my hair. It could be so quiet in that bedsit.

Late in the afternoon I decided to go and get my bike from the electricity substation. I hadn't got round to it before, for various reasons. I left a note for Lars in case he happened to come back early. Then I changed my mind and crumpled it up. I put one of his shirts on, it nearly came down to below my shorts. I was barefoot inside my trainers. I looked into the front gardens along the way, I would have liked a front garden, with boxwood and ivy. The wind got under my shirt and lifted it up, it felt nice and cool.

There were still a lot of skylarks, and a pair of lapwings in the middle of the road. It struck me that I hadn't been in the countryside all summer, only in the town, it was the first time in my life. Many of the fallow fields were bright pink, the fireweed was in season and I thought about the word as I went, it wasn't one you forgot in a hurry. The same with will-o'-the-wisp and horsefly. Washing flapped in a farmhouse garden, a breath of fabric softener in a gust of wind.

My bike was where I'd left it. I decided to cycle around a bit, I didn't know what else to do. The chain rattled as I set off. I went back to the nearest T-junction and turned left, then biked on through the open countryside. I thought about Lars, his face and chest, and then further down. In a month he'd be back at college, I pushed the thought away. I started making a little noise whenever it came to mind, a whistling sound from between my teeth while I shook my head. I could make other thoughts go away like that too. One Sunday morning I'd woken up early and lay in bed looking around the room. My strappy high heels were under the table. We'd had wine the night before and after the first bottle I'd insisted we open another. I'd gone out to the kitchen to get the corkscrew, the driving instructor was wiping a dish. I searched through the drawer. When I found the corkscrew I held it up in the air and slammed the drawer shut. The driving instructor looked at me and I looked back into his eyes just a moment too long. He tipped his head to the side under the light and I held his gaze. He looked like he didn't know what to make of it, but he smiled at me all the same. I smiled back, then turned jauntily on my heels. That Sunday morning I felt ashamed of myself, I made the whistling sound into the duvet. I didn't even like the driving instructor. Eventually Lars woke up and asked if I was feeling sick, and it was almost like I was.

The chain came off at the edge of a wood. I got off and turned the bike upside down, it was a job getting it back on. The oil was all dried up, but I still got my hands dirty. It got on my shorts as well. I wiped my hands with some dock leaves and decided to find my way home next time I came to a signpost. I got on again.

Just after the wood there was a yellow farmhouse with a flagpole at the front. There were cars parked all down the side of the driveway, one of them was the old Volvo. I turned and biked back to the edge of the wood. I laid the bike down on the ground and went in among the trees and stood and watched. I could smell the suckling pig, a faint chinking of glasses came from the garden. A car came into view at a bend and beeped its horn all the way up to the cobbles. There was a slamming of car doors and laughter. A second later the whole party laughed at once, an eruption.

I went back to the bike and tried to pedal home from memory. It fell short and I got lost. There were run-down cottages with open doors and news on the radio. Gulls flocked around an early harvester in the late sun.

When I got back to Haslev I went up to the bedsit to get some money, then biked down to the phone box and rang Dorte. There was no reply. I rang my parents, it was my dad who answered. They were having coffee and had been busy in the greenhouse, there was some trouble with condensation. He asked how things were doing at the teachers' association. I said things were fine and we were probably going to Anholt. Then I ran out of change and told him to give my love. I tried Dorte again, but she still wasn't in. I bought an ice lolly at the corner shop and took it back with me to the bedsit. I lay in bed and ate it. Some rhythmic noises were coming from the next room. I got up and opened the balcony door and tossed the lolly stick into the bushes. I went for a walk. I walked back. I didn't know what to do with myself, or how to go on.

31.

My bungalow needed decorating for Christmas. I bought two bundles of fir branches and tried to join them together in a long garland to go over the front door. I'd seen one in a magazine, with baubles and snow. After about halfway I gave up. My hands and forearms were all scratched from the wire and my nails were broken, it was a stupid idea. I crumpled the unfinished garland and put it out of the way in the shed. As I turned to go back I almost tripped over the abandoned picnic basket. It occurred to me that I could fill it up with the fir branches and put it on the front doorstep, it would do nicely as a Christmas decoration.

The ticket-office guy had been over to see me twice. His name was Knud. The second time he came his girlfriend was at her sister's over on Fyn. I'd bought a tin of olives and a bottle of red wine and put it out on the table with two upturned glasses. As soon as I saw him leave the station I turned the glasses the right way up. I opened the door before he even knocked and led him into the front room. He'd brought four chocolate turtles with him. We had a laugh about that, then we sat down. He took an olive.

'Have you got any music?' he said.

'Only the radio.'

'Don't you listen to music, then?'

'Yes, on the radio.'

'Okay.'

'Do you want some wine?'

'No, thanks.'

'Are you sure?'

'Go on, then. Thanks. Nice olives.'

'They're from Irma. In Copenhagen,' I said.

'Irma, right,' he said, and then he got up and came and put his hand on my neck. We kissed each other. We got down on the floor and knocked over a chair, we pulled and tore, my leg stuck up in the air like a white post. It wouldn't do in the front room without curtains. We hobbled into the bedroom. The Hamburg express came through, a slight distraction in the corner of his eye, then he shook the rest of his trousers off and did his little skip. He'd done it the last time too. I'd thought then it might be first-time nerves. His body was firm and triangular, we thumped against the slats. Apart from that we didn't connect. We flopped apart and sighed separately, it felt better then. We talked about houses as opposed to flats. His girlfriend wanted to move to Vordingborg, she wanted to have a baby as well, that was what frustrated him. When did you know the time was right? If you didn't know, did it mean it wasn't? We fetched the wine and the tin of olives and sat with pillows in our backs and a candle in the windowsill. He was so excited by the new perspective on the trains, it was quite touching. I put my hand on his upper arm.

That was ten days earlier. Now I thought about him more than was good for me, reality was something else. His girlfriend still shook her tea towels out of the kitchen window.

I invited Dorte over for mulled wine. I bought ginger snaps and gingerbread creams from the baker's to go with it, they had three for ten kroner. I ate one on the way back to make sure they were all right. She came over after work, it fitted in with Hardy's badminton. She'd got herself some new clothes, Christmassy trousers with a slight flare and a cardigan. She brought me some walnuts, a whole bag, it was practically a sack. Plus a piece of brie, some honey and two jars of pickled herring.

'In case there's a Christmas party and you need to bring something,' she said. 'Are they having one on your course?'

'Nah,' I said. 'Just drinks, I think.'

'Just as well, it only makes your bum fat, all that food,' she said, and we laughed, she'd just sent a buffet off to Ortved. She'd lost weight herself. It was due to her busy season, she always felt sick in December. That, and the dark. It took it out of her, just getting up in the mornings not being able to see a hand in front of her face. She sat at the table in the kitchen staring out into the darkness with her coffee every morning before six, while Hardy snored like a tractor. She lost her spirit in December, just when it mattered most. People were queuing down the street for her specials, she'd had to take on help.

'A fat little thing, but good as gold,' she said, then took a drag on her cigarette. I could tell she was feeling down. Her look was glazed. She'd been to view a flat on the outskirts of Næstved, a new development by the roundabout.

'I've always liked Næstved, you know that,' she said, and her expressionless eyes grew moist. I went up and put my arm around her, she sniffed and indicated the paper bag from the baker's on the table.

'Let's see what you've got, eh?' she said, and then the

tears came, and she laughed, and opened the bag with one hand and peered inside. 'Gingerbread creams! You've not spent all your money, have you?' she said, dabbing her cheeks with her forearm and smudging her new cardigan with mascara in the process. She rubbed it, and made it worse.

'Oh, look at me,' she said and sniffed hard again. 'I've been wanting to look nice. What a lovely job you've made of the table. It's been such a long day, and I've been so looking forward.'

'Do you want me to do your feet?' I said.

'Ah, would you? No, you mustn't, not now. You must be dead tired.'

'I'll get the bowl. You sit down over there,' I said, and she stood up, her mascara had run under her eyes as well.

'Talking about dying, do you remember Riborg?' she said with her feet in the hot water, it was a story that always cheered us up no end. We ran into Riborg on our bikes one summer at Ganges Bro, it was a Sunday lunchtime and we'd been out picking strawberries. It had nearly been the death of us, the temperature was almost thirty degrees. We'd cycled eighteen kilometres and the only thing we could think about was getting home and having something to drink, we were getting ratty with each other. Riborg was standing there with her bike just before the viaduct, there was a pillow in her wicker basket.

'There's Riborg. Hello, Riborg,' Dorte called out as we rode past, but Riborg waylaid us.

'Wait a minute, Dorte, where are you going?'

We got off our bikes and wheeled them back. She asked about the strawberries. We asked about the pillow, she was just taking it over to someone she knew.

'I lost Jørgen, you know,' she said, and Dorte did, which might have been why we'd just carried on at first. Not that Dorte couldn't talk about death, but there was a long illness to get through before that: failed courses of treatment, an acute kidney infection, frothy urine, a change of medicine that gave renewed hope, then the relapse, fluid retention and failing strength, and then finally the end, as unexpected as death always is, even when you know it's coming, on the kitchen floor at five o'clock on the Tuesday afternoon. Just before dinner. I looked at Dorte and saw the beads of sweat on her upper lip, she was white as a sheet and leaned against her bike for support. Then we got the story all over again, only from a different point of view, starting with Jørgen's physical form before the first and second periods in hospital. Dorte dabbed her lip with the back of her hand, she stood there swaying. I reached out for a big strawberry in her basket and gave it to Riborg. Riborg ate it. It was a good one. I gave her another and her narrative tailed away. We were able to get going again after that. Dorte always thanked me for that move with the strawberry. Riborg, love, she'd been about to say. Death's a terrible thing, but it's time you got a grip.

She sat with her feet in two plastic bags under the table, I'd put the lotion on thick. She groaned when I rubbed it in, her legs were all stiff from her long days in the shop. After the mulled wine I did her nails, she picked a baby-pink polish that matched her slippers.

'Not that there's much point. Hardy won't be seeing my toes much longer anyway,' she said.

'What's he going to do?'

'He doesn't know he needs to do anything yet, I'm afraid.'

'Are you?'

'Am I what?'

'Afraid for him.'

'No. I'm not actually. It's not that at all. It's more me, I'm forty-five now, aren't I?'

'I never think of you as being that old.'

'I don't either, mostly. No, Hardy'll be all right. He's got Samson.'

'Do you want a ginger snap?'

'Thanks,' she said. She bit off a tiny corner, she could hardly swallow it.

Her feet slid around in her shoes from all the lotion. We had a laugh about it and she had another cigarette for the road out on the step. The sky was pitch black, the temperature was down to freezing. In the gap between the flats we could just see the Christmas garland on the main street picked out by the street lights. It swayed faintly.

'There's a guy who works over at the station. In the ticket office,' I said.

'Over there?'

'Yeah. But he lives with someone.'

'That never stopped anyone growing fond.'

'I know. But I don't think I'm that fond, that's the trouble.'

'Well, that's no good. What a pity. Are you sure?'

'I think so.'

'If in doubt, then leave well alone. You have to feel it, right down to your fingertips.'

'Not all the time, surely?'

'Oh, yes. All the time.'

'Who says?'

'I do. So it has to be true, doesn't it? Ha. Take care of

yourself, won't you, love?' she said, and flicked the end of her cigarette onto the lawn. We hugged.

'Thanks for doing my feet. Lovely that, isn't it?' she said with a nod at the picnic basket.

'Some people from Copenhagen left it behind.'

'I'm glad you've made friends there,' she said, and smiled. She stepped on her cigarette end on her way over the grass and bent down to pick it up. She turned and waved before getting into the van.

32.

The summer holiday came to an end. Lars was back at college, only he couldn't get up in the mornings, he kept putting the alarm forward. Other times he turned the clock on its face and pulled the duvet up over his head. I squirmed out of the foot end and opened the balcony door. I put an old T-shirt dress on and went to the kitchen, I made an omelette from a couple of eggs and a sliced tomato. I carried it back into the room together with the coffee and put it on the table, then sat and waited for him to wake up. Every now and then I picked up the alarm clock and made it go off in his face. That really annoyed him. He pushed my arm away and sat up on the edge of the bed.

One Sunday morning over breakfast I told him I was going to write a letter to Per and explain everything. He kept shaking his head.

'I wish you wouldn't,' he said.

'Why not? It's not that bad, surely?' I said. I touched

his neck beneath his ear, his skin was so delicate there. I thought about the word jawline. He always smelled so nice after he'd slept.

'It's worse, it makes me feel ill just thinking about it,' he said, and slapped his hand down on the table. His voice was strangled, emotion welled in his throat. But it was me who started to cry, his hand gave me a fright, it came down right next to mine.

'I'm sorry, darling,' he said. We leaned our heads together. We talked about what we could do. There had to be something. I said we needed to get out together, if only for a little walk down the street.

'You're right,' he said, and a bit later we got dressed. It took us ages, the weather was changeable and he couldn't decide whether to wear shorts or long trousers. I made myself up in front of the balcony door, pink lipstick and a bit of mascara.

'Should I take some money with us?' he said.

'What for?' I said at first, but then the next minute:

'You could do, I suppose. We might want something.'

'I don't think I will,' he said.

'Don't then,' I said.

We went downstairs and out through the yard. The little girls were playing with a watering can. I smiled at them.

'What great watering,' I said, and they looked up at us and smiled back, one of them lifted the watering can up in front of her.

Out on the street we stood for a bit, unable to decide, then went left towards the square. There weren't many people out. A young guy came out of the baker's with two big bags and disappeared round a corner. We didn't speak, all we did was walk. After the station I took his hand, I even began to swing our arms, only he resisted. The wind was chilly, but the sun had come out. I dragged him over to a bench and we sat down. The sun shone in our faces, I closed my eyes. I could hear his breathing. We got up again and went round behind the square through the little lane. A fat woman stood outside a crooked house in her slippers, it was the woman who'd come to my rescue, only without her moped this time. She smiled at us.

'Hello there.'

'Hi,' I said.

'Keeping warm all right?'

'Just about. The wind's a bit chilly,' I said, and she nodded.

'The autumn's here now,' she said as we walked by. I raised my hand in a wave behind my back and gave Lars a squeeze with the other. He hadn't said anything, he didn't until we got home, with rosy cheeks and fresh air in our hair. We took our jumpers off.

'Who was that woman?' he said.

'She's got a moped,' I said.

'I see,' he said, and smiled.

'It was nice to get out together. It didn't hurt a bit,' I said, and smiled back.

But that evening he lost his appetite. He picked at his potato salad, all he ate was half a sausage. He had a lot of reading to do for the following week, he'd hardly even started. He said he found it hard to concentrate in the bedsit when I was there with him. I could see that. I went and sat with my crossword at the wobbly table in the kitchen. The place smelled of something gone off, old meat or cold cuts, but I couldn't get to the bottom of it. There was half a bag of flour with mites in it on a shelf, but that didn't smell at all. I binned it and wiped the shelf. I opened the skylight and had a cup of coffee, then went back into the room, Lars was lying on the daybed with his eyes closed. I sat down. The duvet was warm. I began to touch him. At first he didn't react, then he opened his eyes.

'I can't make you live like this,' he said.

'How do you mean?' I said.

'This. It's no life. Stuck in here or the kitchen.'

'I go into town. And we went for a walk today.'

'I know, but still.'

'I nearly got to Faxe the day before yesterday.'

'Come off it.'

'No, it's true. Anyway, I decide for myself if I've got a life.'

'But it's my life too.'

'Yes, but then it's not a matter of whether you can make me live with it. Then it's you. It's you who doesn't want it.'

'It's not exactly ideal, is it?' he said, not wanting an answer. I turned away slightly and looked out at the night sky as if there was something important there.

'Come here,' he said, and pulled me down on top of him, he chafed the skin on my face with his stubble. I sucked his lower lip in and let go.

'And then there's the cabin trip next weekend, you'll be all on your own,' he said.

'What trip's that?'

'To someone's cabin. I don't even know where it is.'

'The whole class, you mean?'

'That's right.'

It was a strange week. The days ran together. I stood in the shower and thought about gains and losses. Someone kept using my shampoo all the time, the expensive one from the hairdresser's, I had to start hiding it away at the back of the pinewood cupboard. I bought a new jacket for autumn, nylon with a padded lining. Lars said it looked good on me.

I walked round the town in it. They'd started selling flapjacks at the petrol station for some reason. I bought one every day and had it for lunch. I went by the teacher training college. I didn't go in, just stood at the end of the drive and stared. The lawns and benches were deserted. I tried to imagine what went on behind the thick, white walls. A caretaker stood painting a wooden board on two trestles over by an annexe, he waved to me with his brush.

They were going straight after college on the Friday. Lars took his sleeping bag with him that morning, he strapped it onto his pannier rack with an elastic cord. I stood in the kitchen with my head stuck out of the skylight and waved. In the afternoon I went for a walk. I went up to the college and saw him standing in a group in the car park. There weren't that many of them. There was a girl with brown hair in an untucked blouse. She had something in her hand that she lifted up in the air, they all laughed and one of the others tried to snatch it. She jumped in the driver's seat of a white car, so it might have been the car key. The engine started, and the others laughed. There was a chinking of bottles. Lars got in beside her. I turned and went along the edge of some-one's back garden onto a path that led away between two houses. A woman was out walking her dog. It stopped in front of me and I patted it.

When I came home I got my suitcase out of the storage room and packed my things together. I took a piece of paper from a folder but didn't know what to write, I sat and looked around. I'd forgotten the pewter mug, it was on the table with some sprays in it. I took them out into the kitchen, threw them away and wiped the mug. Then I went back and put it in the suitcase, and began to cry. I cried for so long I was exhausted by the time I was finished. I lay down on the daybed and fell asleep. When I woke up it was evening. I went and splashed some cold water on my face, the guy from Egøje was playing Dire Straits. Not long after, I unpacked again and put everything back in its place. I cut two new sprays in the dim light of the yard.

A week later it was Lars's turn to write. I found his letter in my crossword magazine when I came back from a tanning session late Friday afternoon. He said he was very sorry and that he'd moved back home to his parents' until I found somewhere else. He wasn't well, and now he had a doctor's word for it. He didn't know what more to say, he said to look after myself.

I opened the cupboard and sure enough most of his clothes were gone. It felt like a relief, only I didn't know why. It hurt a lot too. I kept standing there staring at the half-empty shelves.

33.

I found some lemon juice in a bottle in the communal kitchen. I mixed it with sugar and Bacardi, it tasted all right. I made a list of all my options on the back of the letter from Lars with a thick black pen. The world opened up as I wrote. But then I started crying anyway, I let my whole face go and stuck my lower lip out like a child. I punched the daybed, but it didn't help, it was a foam mattress. I put some music on and sang along, I sang louder and louder and started to dance about from the corner unit to the door and back. It was like the dancing made me drunk on its own. Then there was a knock on the door, it was the driving instructor, he wanted to know if there was anything the matter. I said we were going out on the town and we'd be quiet now. That was all right then, he said.

I did my make-up and put the yellow dress on, it was a bit too summery, so I put a cardigan on top, with black tights and the strappy high heels, a little beaded clutch bag and my nylon jacket. I felt daft standing in the bar with a whisky. Mostly because of the clutch, but I couldn't stand whisky either. I drank it in one go and ordered another. A guy in a lumberjacket nodded appreciatively across the counter. I looked away. I tried to look like someone who had plans. Two guys beside me laughed, I asked what they were laughing at, they said I looked like a bumblebee. One of them asked for a dance, but I said I didn't feel like it. After the fourth whisky I collected myself and went out into the street. I fell over a cobblestone and grazed my hand and knee. I got to my feet and walked on. A young man called out to me from a parked car, he got out and came over with half a hot dog in his hand. He was in a suit.

'Did you hurt yourself?'

'No, I'm all right.'

'Is anything wrong?'

'No,' I said, and began to cry, then nodded and waved my hand dismissively at the same time.

'It's been a rubbish day, that's all. I'm sorry. Thanks.'

'Can I give you a lift somewhere?'

'No, really, I'm fine.'

'Maybe you should sit down for a minute. Over there,' he said, and pointed to a bench under a street lamp. He put his free arm around my shoulder and helped me across.

It felt very protective. The suit looked good on him, it made him look older than he probably was.

'I like your suit,' I said.

'Thanks.'

'Have you been to work?'

'No, I've been at a party. Not for very long, though, it was a rubbish party.'

We laughed. I sniffed. He finished his hot dog in a couple of mouthfuls and handed me the napkin.

'Here,' he said.

'Thanks,' I said. I blew my nose, then dabbed under my eyes.

'No, it was a decent party, really,' he said. 'I was tired, that's all, so I left. Now I'm off home to get some sleep.'

'Do you live here in Haslev?'

'Just outside. Do you?'

'Yes. Well, no, I'm moving.'

'Oh, I see.'

'I'll probably try to find somewhere in Næstved.'

'Næstved's nice.'

'It's lively, anyway.'

'It is. Do you fancy half a Cocio? I'll go and get it,' he said, and went back to the car. He came back with the bottle of chocolate milk and offered it to me, it hadn't been touched. I took a swig.

'That's good,' I said. 'I've had a bit too much whisky.'

'I know how you feel.'

'Once I had too much apple schnapps,' I said, and we laughed again, he was actually quite good-looking. The door of the bar opened. Loud music, then someone came out into the street and whistled, possibly at us. They disappeared round a corner and the door closed again.

'It was kind of you to come and see if I was okay,' I said.

'Don't mention it. I'd still like to drive you home.'

'There's no need. I only live around the corner.'

'Maybe I could you walk you home, then?'

'That'd be nice,' I said, and got to my feet. My head started swimming. He got up as well and put his protective arm under mine. We walked over the cobbles, him with the Cocio and me with my clutch. A wobbling cyclist went past as we reached the lane. He took my hand and helped me down from the high kerb. We crossed the road, still holding on to each other.

'Is it this way?' he said, and I nodded.

'You're very nice.'

'Thanks. What's your name?'

'Dorte.'

'I'm Leon.'

'Are you?'

'Yes,' he said, and then we'd reached the corner shop,

there was a bundle of newspapers on the step. We stopped and looked at them, they were from the day before.

'It's an unusual name,' I said.

'I know, I don't know any other Leons,' he said, and then he smiled at me. We looked into each other's eyes for a while.

'Anyway, this is where I live,' I said.

A narrow alley ran behind the shop. It didn't look like somewhere anyone would live.

'Down there?'

'Yes. Thanks a lot for your help.'

'Pleasure,' he said. Then he stepped forward and kissed me on the cheek.

'Look after yourself, now.'

He stood there as I walked off down the alley. The yard behind the shop was full of clutter, I hid in between two skips and waited. I was freezing in my yellow dress, a rustling sound kept coming from one of the skips. After a bit I went back and looked. He was gone. I crossed over the street and hurried home.

34.

I lived in a bedsit in Haslev. I had a daybed with storage, and a corner unit and a desk with a pewter mug on it. In the mornings I went to the baker's for a poppy-seed twist and a roll. I ate them at the desk and got crumbs everywhere. I brushed the crumbs into my hand and tossed them out of the balcony door. I didn't do much cooking, I didn't like being in the kitchen any more. The driving instructor had found himself a girlfriend, she was pretty and thin. She put her make-up on with the door open and was always packing stuff into sports bags. She kept her toiletries in the bathroom. She had a wheatgerm facial mask, I tried it out and put too much on. I lay on the daybed and read *Amerika*. I wrote a story about a woman who was dead, and took the bus to Stevns. I bought a packet of cigarettes and smoked them, I didn't like the taste.

The guy from Egøje asked after Lars, he wanted to borrow his soldering iron. I told him Lars was on a cabin trip, but I would try to find the soldering iron for him. I found it in the storage room, only it was an immersion heater instead. He said it didn't matter, he could make do with a lighter. He asked if I wanted a bag of muesli for nothing. He'd bought it himself, but there was too much bran in it, it was like having a mouthful of dust. He was wearing a blue vest and asked me in for a beer. We drank with our feet up on the coffee table. It was painted orange, he'd made it himself, a long time ago in woodwork. He had a hologram on the wall above the TV, he'd spent a whole month's wages on it. It was a skull. We watched a detective drama, then got down on the carpet. He had a way of touching my stomach. It was all nice and relaxed. I watched TV with him in the evenings. After a few weeks he asked about Lars. I told him Lars was on that cabin trip. Long cabin trip, he said. His girlfriend was an au pair in Paris, he didn't know quite what to make of it. He was thinking of going down there, he'd have to see. He cut his own fringe, it was nearly straight. When my birthday came round he gave me a bracelet. It was from a proper jeweller's, it came in a box. I had to give it a few more weeks after that, and by then it was nearly *his* birthday, he made a point about birthdays. I gave him an anchor-link chain in sterling silver and we ate out at a restaurant. He had Wiener schnitzel, I had something in mushroom sauce. On the way home we had a beer in a bar and played a game of dice. No sound came out when he laughed. His cigarette smoke curled between his teeth.

At the end of the year I got a letter from Lars. He'd given up the lease on the room so I'd have to move out. He sounded like he wasn't well. I need some peace and quiet, he wrote. His writing slanted heavily to the left, it didn't normally, but he'd drawn his usual face beneath his name, even if it wasn't smiling. Not long after, I saw him from the back seat of a bus striding briskly along a street holding hands with the brown-haired girl, they had a little white dog with them. I turned and looked back, the dog squatted under a street lamp. They tugged on its lead, they looked like they were happy. It was a diverted route, somewhere between Næstved and Ringsted, I'd moved in with Dorte again. I could hardly breathe the rest of the way. When eventually we got to Ringsted, I got off two stops early and ran all the way home. Dorte was in the front room watching TV. I went to the bathroom and cried for ages into a towel. After that I felt better. We lived quietly for about eight months. We baked cakes and played cards, and put highlights in each other's hair with crochet hooks. I wrote words for party songs meant for no one and applied for my course. I was planning to get the train from Ringsted every day, but then Hardy came along and I moved out into the bungalow.

35

In February I ran into Hase at Scala. He was having egg and chips. I recognised him from the curve of his back, he reached out for the tomato sauce and gave it a good shake. I stood watching him. I was about to go on, but then he turned and saw me. He got up and we gave each other a little hug. I'd bought two hair slides, they were in a carrier bag that was far too big for them. He pointed at it.

'Out shopping?'

'Sort of.'

'I'm just having some breakfast.'

'It looks good.'

'Do you want some? They do toasted sandwiches as well.'

'No, thanks. I've just eaten.'

'A coffee, then. They make a decent cup here. Have a seat,' he said, and held his hand out towards the table. I put my bag on a chair and sat down.

'What do you fancy? Cappuccino? Au lait?'

'Olé,' I said, and he nodded a bit awkwardly.

'I'll go up and get you one.'

He still had food on his plate, now it was getting cold while he queued up at the counter. He was taller than I remembered him, but just as round-shouldered. It looked like there was something wrong with the coffee machine, the girl had to call for assistance, people stood shuffling in the queue. He was reading a paperback, *Madame Bovary*, it was on the table with the back cover facing up and a yellow bookmark sticking out. His coat hung from the back of his chair. He looked down from where he stood and sent me a smile. He'd grown his hair since the last time I'd seen him. After a while they got the coffee sorted and he came down with it on a little tray.

'That's really nice of you. Your breakfast'll be cold now,' I said.

'Ah, it doesn't matter. What have you been doing with yourself, anyway?'

'Not a lot.'

'Do you see much of the Oldies?' he said, and we had a laugh. I took too big a sip of my coffee and gulped some air down with it, I choked and had to swallow some more.

'Not really. Do you?' I said, and he shook his head.

'No, I stopped, didn't I?'

'Did you?'

'Did you stop as well, then?'

'Yes, sort of. Or rather I never really started,' I said, and we had a good laugh about that as well. He cut his fried egg and the yolk ran out. My throat felt funny after that mouthful of coffee that had gone the wrong way, I couldn't control my voice properly.

'It was a bit of a daft name for a reading group,' I said.

'I know, you're not that old, are you?'

'Twenty-one.'

'I'm twenty-five, so it was all right for me. My birthday was yesterday, as a matter of fact.'

'Was it? Happy birthday.'

'That's why I'm having breakfast now. Bit of a late night.'

'Were you out on the town?'

'No, just out for a meal with an old trumpeter friend and then a few drinks after that.'

'Do you play the trumpet?'

'You must be joking,' he said, and we laughed again, he put his knife and fork down and pushed his plate away.

'But you do sing in a choir,' I said.

'Not any more, not since I moved from Greve. I took on my brother's cooperative flat on Enghavevej this autumn,' he said, and I nodded. All I did was sit and nod.

'Vesterbro,' he said.

'I know,' I said.

He'd taken up smoking, it didn't look right on him. He blew the smoke downwards diagonally, his exhalations were very efficient. He told me about the flat, it was above a bicycle shop, which was good because he always had a flat tyre. I couldn't really see him on a bike. His share in the cooperative had cost eleven thousand, he'd had to think about it because he'd planned on going to Ecuador, he couldn't afford to do both. I couldn't see him in Ecuador either. He leaned across the table in his jumper and smiled at me.

'Fancy a beer?' he said.

'Isn't it a bit early?'

'Who's stopping us?' he said, and went up to get two large ones. He took his dirty plate and cutlery back with him, it made him look like a regular. I wondered why I'd never come across him there before if he was. Perhaps he took his plate back wherever he went. The beers were huge, I didn't know how I'd ever manage to get it all down, or what we'd have to talk about, but by the time I'd drunk half we were doing quite well. He told me about his brother and growing up in Karlslunde. He asked about where I'd gone to school. His father had been his class teacher, it had been awkward at times, but after year seven he changed schools. The headmaster's name was Grauballe, they called him The Grauballe Man, after the bog body, even the teachers, as if it wasn't obvious enough, but Hase didn't cotton on until years later. How stupid could you get. His brother was a doctor now, he'd been a model student, he'd even done the flat up while he'd been taking his finals. He was the kind of person who sanded things down and used primer, it was sickening really. But now Hase was reaping the rewards.

'You'll have to come and see me sometime,' he said.

'Yes,' I said.

'I'll do a turkey stew. I'm good at turkey stew,' he said.

I went to the bathroom. I had no idea what the time was. The good baker's at Central Station had cream buns for Lent, I'd planned to get one on the way home and hoped I wouldn't forget. I splashed water on my face, then remembered I was wearing foundation and dabbed myself dry with a paper towel. It didn't matter about that bun. But I'd get the next train, if there was time, or the one after that.

Hase had got more beer in when I got back. There was no way I'd be able to drink it, I didn't know how to tell him. I steered myself down onto my chair. *Madame Bovary* was gone, probably in his rucksack. He sat with his head in his hands, his hair flopped forward a bit.

'Did you know I'm a poet now?' he said.

'A poet?' I said.

'Yeah, since November. The nineteenth, to be exact,' he said with a small grin, and scratched his throat. He'd started going to a poetry club in the autumn where it was open mic, at first he'd just sat and listened to the others, but then in November he'd plucked up the courage and put his name down to read. His hands had been so sweaty the paper got wet while he was waiting for his turn. The poem was called 'Fugue for Meat'. He was already out of breath as he made his way up to the little stage, he was on after an elderly man in a leather hat. It was a funny thing about those leather hats. Whenever there was something arty on there would always be at least one. Not that he'd call his own poem art. The organiser took the microphone and introduced him.

'And now we're going to listen to Poet Hase.'

'Poet Hase,' I said.

'I know,' he said, and we laughed. The reading had gone down well, everyone applauded.

'I'd like to read that poem,' I said.

'No, you wouldn't. It's no good.'

'But they applauded.'

'They always applaud,' he said, and took a slurp of his

beer. I did the same, the afternoon went, and in the evening we had cajun food on the second floor, gumbo and pecan pie. After that we went to the Irish pub. We spent all our money, and somewhere along the way I forgot my carrier bag with the hair slides in it, but that didn't matter much. I could buy some more the next time. They weren't very expensive.

36.

I was sleeping a bit better at night. I'd found a technique of sitting up yawning for an hour before going to bed. I let fresh air into the bedroom, and when I got under the covers I repelled intrusive thoughts by saying 'Right you are'. I still kept waking up a lot in the night, though. As soon as I found myself thinking the thought that I was awake, I knew I might as well get up. I went and got a glass of water or a piece of bread and sat in the front room looking across at the station. Sometimes there was a light on in the flat, I took it for granted it was Knud who was up. He had so many worries about his future. In principle he would have given his girlfriend whatever she wanted, she'd always been there for him one hundred per cent, she'd literally saved his life, he said. She'd fetched him home from Cosy Bar when he'd passed out in a corner and had lost his shoe. The biggest problem was her coldness, he said, she could be so cold. His own body was burning hot, it was one of his best attributes. He could really warm my bed up, usually it was freezing. When I was on my own and couldn't sleep, I carried the duvet into the utility room and draped it over the boiler. Then I would lean up against the radiator in the front room and sit in the dark looking out. One night I saw a movement over by the bushes in the light from the lamp post. I put my bread down and went and opened the door. I padded a little way down the path in my bare feet, I was just about to say something soppy. Only it wasn't Knud's white dressing gown, this one was green, a little puff of smoke curled in the air around it. His girlfriend was standing with a cigarette, she heard me and turned round.

'Oh, hi,' I said.

'Hi,' she said, and took another drag.

I didn't know what to pretend I was doing there on the garden path. I breathed in and out. My breath was white, the air was so cold it hurt inside my nose. I made to go inside again, but then she spoke to me.

'I don't smoke,' she said.

'Oh, right,' I said.

A few moments went by. I looked up at the sky. There wasn't much to see.

'I can't sleep,' she said after a bit.

'Me neither,' I said, but she didn't seem to be listening, she closed her eyes.

'I've got to be at work in four hours, we've got performance evaluations, I'm absolutely knackered,' she said.

She had pyjama pants on under her dressing gown and a pair of furry boots with suede laces, I'd got some the same that I'd bought on the Strøget.

'That must be hard on you,' I said, a bit indistinctly, I had to clench my teeth so they wouldn't start chattering.

'Anyway,' she said as if she was about to go, only then she stayed put. She took a drag on her cigarette then tossed it away.

'I've got the same boots as you,' I said.

We both looked at them, she didn't answer. She gathered her dressing gown. I was frozen stiff by this point. I ventured a smile.

'Well, I'd better go back in where it's warm.'

'I'm sorry if I gave you a fright,' she said.

'No, it's all right, you didn't.'

'I didn't mean to.'

'Don't worry about it, really.'

'Okay.'

'Right you are,' I said with a nod, then turned and went back in to what passed for warmth. I took the duvet off the boiler and scrambled into bed. After a long time the Gedser train came clattering through, so it was half past five. I got up and made toast and put some coffee on. I looked across at the flat. At half past six a light came on, first in the living room, then in the kitchen, then after that someone opened the bathroom window. At quarter past seven the light went off again and another one came on downstairs in the ticket office. I fell asleep at about half past eight and woke up well into the afternoon, but it didn't matter. I had no plans.

37

Hase sent me a postcard inviting me over for turkey on the Sunday evening, not stew, but a leg. *It's in the fridge and it's huge,* he wrote. We were going to eat early and then go to the open-mic night at the poetry club in town. He would expect me around six. He'd written his address down one edge, down the other he'd written WE'RE WAITING FOR SOMEONE in small capitals. There was a photo of an owl on the front, I thought it was quite exotic. I went to the bookshop and the supermarket to find a card I could send back with a reply, but all they had were novelty and birthday cards with pre-printed messages. I made my own instead, from the cardboard backing of an A4 notepad, I frayed the edges and used a black marker pen. Then I decided to shade the letters, but that only ruined it. I ended up finding an old Christmas card at the back of a folder, there was a little sparrow on it, so it was a good match for the owl. I wrote in pencil, casually and with a light hand, then more distinctly at the bottom: BUT FOR WHOM I WONDER. I thought better of that bit later on when I couldn't sleep, and then I couldn't sleep at all. It was Friday, music was coming from the pub, upbeat jazz and a chorus of raucous voices joining in on a repeated line, bitter-sweet something. It had me missing Knud. I tossed and turned, eventually I got up and went into the front room, but their flat was all dark. I cut a couple of slices off a cob loaf and listened to the radio. I sat by the lamp and tried to write a poem. I wanted it to be called 'Novices'. Someone coughed heavily outside in the street, a rattle of mucus. It was a group from the pub, off to catch the last train. One of them caught sight of me and waved, a little man with a beard, I waved back on a reflex. They all waved then, and carried on until they disappeared round the other side of the station building. I felt uplifted, I sat there with a smile on my face. When I went back to bed I kept seeing all their waving hands in my mind's eye and thought about the gesture. The fact that raised hands could make you feel wanted, special almost, even if you weren't. Just as you were sitting there in your slippers behind a single pane, with a shaky stanza in your head.

It really was a huge turkey leg. He hadn't got round to putting it in the oven when I arrived, he'd fallen asleep in the afternoon. He didn't wake up until I rang the bell just after six, he could hardly get himself together. His hair was dishevelled, there was a red blotch on his cheek.

'How stupid,' he said.

We were standing by the worktop. It was a nice kitchen, he had plants in the window behind the sink, a fern and some chives, and a cuckoo clock above the fridge.

'It doesn't matter. What a funny clock,' I said.

'It's kitsch,' he said, and I nodded.

'Oh right.'

Then I looked at the leg again.

'Can't we just put it in now?' I said.

'Yeah, let's. I don't suppose it needs more than an hour.'

'That'll be fine, then.'

'Yeah. We can have some wine while we're waiting.'

We sat down in the living room, he took the sofa and I got the old wicker chair with the blanket. He'd lit a candle in the windowsill, the flame flickered. Muffled sounds came up from the street, cars and a horn, a voice shouting, another shouting back. Then came a sharp hiss that stopped abruptly.

'That's just someone getting air,' he said.

'How do you mean?'

'From the bike shop.'

'Oh, I see. Aren't they closed?'

'Yeah, but it's outside.'

'Oh right,' I said.

We drank the wine I brought with me. It was French, something with Michel in it. It tasted okay. I sat thinking I ought to stop saying *oh right* all the time. He drew his legs up on the sofa, there was a hole in his sock.

'Are you writing at all?' he said.

'No. Are you?'

'Yeah, but nothing good. I sit up half the night with it and never get to bed.'

'I know how it is.'

'Do you?'

'No, I meant not sleeping.'

'Oh right,' he said.

The blotch on his cheek had gone, only now it felt as though my own cheeks were flushing like mad. My glass was nearly empty, I leaned forward and filled it up again. I filled his too, and we drank.

'Are you cold?' he said.

'No. Just a bit.'

'Put the blanket around you, if you want.'

'It doesn't matter. Nice floorboards you've got.'

'My brother did them. Sanded them down, that is.'

'Oh right. He did a good job,' I said.

He found a packet of penne in the kitchen, we were both really hungry and the dinner was taking for ever. There was a good smell from the oven, but the leg was still raw inside, he'd just had a look. We tucked in to the pasta and had another glass of wine. I had a feeling it was late, but it didn't seem like we were in a hurry.

'Are you going to be reading tonight?' I said.

'No. I've got nothing to read. Are you?'

'You must be joking.'

'You never know.'

'No, but I'm looking forward to listening. I've never heard anyone read before.'

'Haven't you?'

'Only Ib Michael.'

'Yeah?'

'He came to our school.'

'Oh right.'

'Have you noticed we both say "Oh right" a lot?' I said. He looked at me and smiled.

'We do, don't we?' he said, and we had a good laugh about it, we couldn't stop, and then we drank the rest of the wine. There was a really good smell of roast turkey now. He realised he'd forgotten the side dishes, we were meant to have a rice salad, but he hadn't even started it yet. He skidded out into the kitchen on his sock with the hole in it. I went with him, but he'd only got brown rice, it needed forty minutes to cook.

'Any idea what the time is?' he said, and I shook my head. I looked up at the cuckoo clock, but it was only for show. 'It's quarter to eight,' he shouted from the bedroom, we had to get going. I turned off the oven and took the leg out. I put it on the hob, it was spitting fat. We pulled our coats on, his keys jangled as we went down the stairs. When we got outside he took my hand and we ran left, zigzagging between some people with suitcases before crossing the road. Then he stopped. He didn't know which bus we had to get, he was always on his bike and didn't know the routes. The air was cold and damp, I thought it might rain.

'We'll get a taxi,' he said, and stopped one almost straight away, all he did was hold up his hand. We were out of breath when we got into the back, we began to laugh again. I could smell the turkey on our coats. I told him, and he sniffed his shoulder.

Apart from us there were only five others there, including the man in the leather hat and the two organisers. They stood on the stage with Cokes in their hands, they looked just like each other, both of them short-haired and wearing jumpers. Hase went to get us some wine. The leather-hat man and a girl at the table nearest the stage sat hunched over their papers. A young couple in black coats came in at the last minute, each with a carrier bag. They sat down quickly. Then the lights were dimmed and a spot lit up the stage. Hase came back with two glasses of wine just as one of the organisers stepped up to the microphone and welcomed the evening's readers and the audience. The girl at the front table was going to read first, she had ordinary jeans on. She adjusted the mic. Hase whispered that her poems had recently been accepted by a publisher. She had finely shaped eyebrows and said she was going to read a poem dedicated to a friend from Sweden. She stood and breathed for a bit, then she began. Her voice was deep and calm. My eyes filled with tears nearly straight away. At first I blinked madly, then I just let them go. She read three poems in all and used the word substance more than twice. I sat completely still in the dim light. When she was finished, she smiled and nodded and went quickly back to her seat and we all applauded loudly. I sniffed as we clapped. Hase leaned forward and looked at me. I took a sip of wine and when I put the glass down he stroked my arm.

Later, after the readings, we went somewhere else, to a cafe with big windows facing the street. We bought peanuts and a whole bottle of red wine. I could see myself behind his back in the mirror on the wall. My face was streaked, but it didn't matter. We talked about living in Copenhagen and about writing seriously, he said next time I should read something for him. I said I might be able to remember something off by heart. As we walked along Vesterbrogade much later it started to rain. We stood under an awning outside a jeweller's and then I recited some of what I remembered. Afterwards he put his arm under mine and led me across the street, my legs were a bit wobbly. We went back to his and opened another bottle of wine, we had the turkey leg with bread and butter. I fell asleep on his sofa with the blanket over me and didn't wake up until mid-morning. There was a note on the coffee table, he'd gone to the dentist's and I should make myself at home. Before I left, I wrote on the back of it: *See you, lots of love.*

38.

Much to my surprise, the front garden had come alive with white and yellow crocuses peeping up from the tiny lawn and under all the bushes. The sun was out and I swept the path. The ten o'clock had just gone, a lone passenger had got off and trudged past with her bag. She nodded towards the lawn.

'What a lot of life.'

'Yes, isn't there?' I said, and smiled at her. Then I saw Knud on the step of the station building waving me over. I left the brush and ambled across. He folded his arms in front of his chest.

'Fancy a coffee?'

'Yes, why not.'

'Come on, then,' he said, and I followed him through the back door into the little office behind the counter. He pulled me to one side and began to kiss me on the throat and then my neck.

'Do you want something to go with that coffee?' he said in a breathy voice, and I did. I looked out of the window at the platform, there wasn't a soul.

'The next one's not due for fifty minutes,' he said, his trousers already down.

'That can't be right. There's one any minute.'

'That's a through train.'

'Since when?'

'Since today.'

'Is there a new timetable?'

'No, it's just for this week.'

'How come?'

'I don't know. Nobody tells us anything.'

'But what are people supposed to do?'

'What people?'

'Passengers.'

'There aren't any. There never are for the ten-twelve.'

'Never?'

'That's right.'

'Suppose I wanted to get on?'

'You never go that way.'

'No, but what if I did?'

'Well, you couldn't,' he said, and then the train came. He was right, it was a through train, it whistled past with its long trail of carriages. A white carrier bag flew up from the platform and settled again a bit further away.

We had the coffee afterwards. I sat on the edge of the little desk and looked across at my bungalow. The windows were all open, I'd wanted to get some air in all of a sudden and freshen the place up, it was the same reason I'd been sweeping the path. There were some clothes soaking in the bath, tops and socks that would dry on the line in the back garden. He sat on the swivel chair and put his hand on my knee.

'You're up early today,' he said.

'No earlier than usual.'

'You sleep later, normally.'

'No, I don't.'

'You'll be having yourself a nice long snooze now,' he said. I slapped his hand, the one he had on my knee, and he slapped back. He gulped some coffee, then he wiped his mouth.

'I've applied to become a guard,' he said suddenly.

'You haven't? What sort of a guard?'

'On the trains, of course.'

'Starting when?'

'I don't know yet. I've applied, that's all.'

'It sounds like a good opportunity.'

'Yeah, I think it is.'

'You won't be able to keep an eye on me all day from the office, though. You'll have to make do with looking over from the flat,' I said.

'We'd have to move as well,' he said.

'Move? Where to?'

'Looks like Høje Taastrup, at the moment. Hanne's from there originally.'

'I see,' I said.

'Are you upset?' he said.

'Not really. I've got nothing against Høje Taastrup.'

'You needn't be. It won't be until summer. Perhaps we can write to each other.'

'Ha, ha.'

'What's funny about that?' he said with wounded emphasis, it made me feel sorry for him, his firm, triangular body on the swivel chair with his polo shirt untucked. He ran his fingers once through his hair. I smiled at him.

'Nothing. Of course we can.'

When I got back to the bungalow the door had blown shut. I stood on the step and rattled the handle, my key was inside. It must have been the draught, all the open windows. I fetched a rusty garden chair and placed it under the bedroom window. I opened the window all the way and wriggled my way over the ledge and straight into bed. I decided to stay there. I wasn't really upset, it was just the abrupt change of situation, from standing with him inside me to sitting apart and being informed about Høje Taastrup in the space of a few minutes. As he'd predicted, I slept well into the afternoon, then when I woke up I went out and picked a handful of crocuses. I went over to the station with them, he was cashing up, his girlfriend was standing next to him in her baggy jumper. They both looked up at me in surprise, I handed her the flowers.

'Here,' I said. Her face softened and her mouth widened slightly.

'What are they for?' she said.

'I've got so many,' I said.

39

My savings account was empty. To keep my spending down
I'd started taking a packed lunch with me to Copenhagen.
I ate on a bench on Axeltorv looking across at Scala. They'd
put tables and chairs out now, when the weather was nice
people sat with burgers and ice-cream sundaes. I saw
nothing of Hase. I'd sent him a postcard from the Bicycle
and Moped Museum thinking it was better than the last
one, but he hadn't replied. I had a sandwich or a pitta
bread with me and some water in a bottle. After I'd eaten
I sometimes went into Scala and bought a bag of pick 'n'
mix, the smallest I could get away with. I walked up and
down the Strøget and went round the narrow streets behind
Rådhuspladsen, then along Vesterbrogade with my canvas
bag hanging down at my side. It went dark brown in the
rain. They sold cheap ankle boots next to the Føtex supermarket. I found a pair in my size and wore them straight
away, they put my old shoes in a bag for me. Vesterbrogade

seemed endless. I bought a big chocolate-covered marzipan bar at an overpriced kiosk. There was a hint of warmth in the air, it swirled between the buildings and rose up off the pavement. A man cycled past with a lamp, a woman called after him. I dumped the bag with my old shoes in it in a bin where the street came to an end. Then I went back along the opposite pavement. I turned right down Enghavevej to the bicycle shop and went up to Hase's. I rang his bell, but there was no answer. I pushed the marzipan bar through the letter box, it landed on something that sounded like a newspaper.

Back on Vesterbrogade I discovered I'd got a blister on my heel, but it was too far to the bin I'd dumped my shoes in. I might not have liked rummaging around for them anyway. I limped along bit by bit. At Central Station I went into the chemist's for some plasters. There was a long queue and I missed the four o'clock. I waited for the next one by the stairs to the platform. I bought a hot dog and a small bar of nougat that I ate on the train. I sat falling asleep with my head against the window. The curtains always had the same smell, fuel of some kind, or tar.

The sun was low at the end of the road when I hobbled home from the station with an ankle boot in my hand. The postman had been, there were three letters. One from the bank telling me I was in the red. One from someone I didn't know saying Dorte had gone into hospital with what you weren't supposed to call a nervous breakdown any more. She was feeling a lot better now and I wasn't to worry. I could go and see her, there was an address and a ward number, and two hundred kroner in a square of tinfoil. And then a postcard in a thick envelope from Hase, it was from Prague, he was there with an old friend. He was coming home on the Friday and wanted to take me round Søndermarken on the Saturday if I felt like it. That was tomorrow. I sat on the step and felt unstuck. The ankle boot was on the doormat, I still had the other one on. I sat like that for some time, trying to separate things. If I smoked I would have smoked. I did want to go to Søndermarken.

40.

Dorte was sitting in her room on the ward in a woolly jumper and a pair of jeans, all the way there I'd been picturing her in a hospital gown. She sat at a little table with a mug and a cigarette, and looked up when she heard me come in.

'Oh hello, love. How nice of you. Come and sit down.'

There was only the one chair in the room. She got halfway to her feet, but I shook my head.

'No, don't get up.'

'Are you sure?' she said. Her clothes hung miserably from her frame. She sat down again with her cigarette.

'You sit on the bed, then,' she said. 'I hope you've not brought anything.'

'I haven't.'

'That's all right, then. There's some peppermints in the drawer, do you want one?'

'No, thanks.'

'There's chewing gum as well.'

'No, thanks. How are you feeling?'

'Oh, coming along, I think,' she said.

'How do you mean?'

'Just coming along, that's all.'

I looked out of the window. There was a big lawn and flowerbeds with blue perennials, and birch trees with still, bare branches. Beyond lay the fjord, white and calm as a millpond. The bus I'd taken had gone right along the edge, the only passengers had been me and two young girls. They kept sniggering about something one of them had in her bag.

'Who sent me the letter?' I said.

'What letter? I don't know about any letter,' said Dorte.

'There was two hundred kroner in it.'

'That'd be Andy, then. He's been such a help.'

'Is he from England?'

'No, he's in the kitchen.'

'Here, you mean?'

'Yes, you can go and say hello.'

'Okay.'

'You should.'

'I will, then.'

'Yes, do. Look out for his cheekbones,' she said.

He wasn't in the kitchen, he was in the lounge wiping the windowsill with a cloth. He turned and smiled.

'Hello, there,' he said.

'Hi. I'm here visiting Dorte. She's my aunt,' I said.

'Oh, so you're the one,' he said, pulling off a rubber glove and extending his hand. 'Nice of you to stop by.'

'Thanks for sending that letter.'

'Don't mention it.'

'How long's she been here?'

'Oh, ten or twelve days. She's coming along fine now.'

'She seems a bit confused to me.'

'Do you think so? It might be the medication. She's not off it yet.'

'Why was she brought in?'

'She was in a state. Not very well at all.'

'Had something happened?'

'No, nothing in particular, as far as I know. Sometimes it just happens, bang.'

'How did she get here?'

'As I understand it, your parents came with her. At least, I think it was them.'

'I'm sure,' I said.

'Could that be right? I can ask to look in the record.'

'No need,' I said. 'Thanks for helping her and everything.'

I went to the bathroom and drank some water. Everywhere was so clean and deserted. Dorte's mug was empty when

I went back to her room. I poured her some more coffee in the corridor and some for myself. There was some Battenberg on a plate and I took two pieces, one for Dorte and one for me. I got her to have a bite and talk about what happened.

'I'd just made a tuna mousse, with gelatine. And then I dropped the whole lot.'

'You poor thing.'

'On the floor, you know. I didn't know what to do.'

She shook her head.

'I just stood there looking at it. Odd, don't you think? I couldn't move. There seemed to be tuna mousse everywhere. Then I felt so frightened.'

'I understand.'

'Do you? Anyway, the shop's going to be so nice now, your dad's going to paint it for me. It'll brighten the place up no end. And your mum.'

Before I left we sat on the edge of the bed together. We looked out at the white fjord, she leaned her head against mine.

'Are you getting on all right?' she said.

'Yes, I'm fine.'

We spoke very softly, we were sitting so close together.

'Have you got exams?' she said.

'Now, you mean? No, not yet.'

'That's nice. You can take things easy, then.'

'Yes, I suppose.'

She patted my thigh, then her own.

'I've been meaning to give you these trousers. They're no good on me any more.'

'I think they'd be too small for me.'

'Do you think so? We'll have them let out, then.'

'I didn't think you could let jeans out.'

'Oh, yes. You can put a gusset in.'

'That's kind of you.'

'I can't very well do without them here, but once I get home they're yours. Proper Levi's they are, from Bilka.'

'Thanks.'

'We could do a Bilka trip one day.'

'Yes, we could.'

'I'd like that.'

When I reached the stop, the bus had already gone eight minutes earlier and there was an hour and a half until the next one was due. The gulls soared silently over the fjord. I started to walk, I wasn't bothered.

41.

All through April I stayed in Glumsø. I slept when I could. I ate, and sat at my table. In the afternoons I'd go for a walk. I walked further and further along the road before turning back. I never came across anyone I knew. The grain was growing in the fields now, skylarks ascended in bursts, the plum trees were in blossom. A new charity shop had opened next to the bookshop, I was there every other day, rummaging through the bins. It was mostly tablecloths and pillowcases they got in, not at all like in Copenhagen. I bought a length of material with lemons on it, but ended up throwing it out. Knud stood on the step in the sun in his breaks, he waved across at me. They'd already started clearing out and packing. They'd taken an old bookcase apart, it stuck up out of the skip in the car park. I put my rusty garden chair out under the apple tree in the front garden and sat there turning brown to match. Sometimes I saw a face looking at me from the window of a train.

There was an intense exchange of postcards with Hase, starting with one he sent me from Søndermarken. *Seeing as how you never came*, he wrote. *I'll be coming soon*, I replied. *Do*, he wrote back, *I'm looking forward to seeing you again, I've got an extra bike and a trench coat, we'll go to Hvidovre and watch the lights come on. I'd rather sit on the back*, I wrote, *then I can hold on to your trench coat, I'm not keen on cycling in the city. Sounds good, but Hvidovre's not the city, you've a lot to learn*, he wrote, and then after that: *I've met someone you should meet, she lives in Vanløse, that's not the city either. She wants to look at our work with us. She's nearly a proper writer, she goes to a writers' school. You'd never believe it, but I met her in Scala. What work? I haven't got any work*, I wrote. *She can meet with us on May the tenth*, he wrote, *she's got room in her diary then. It would mean a lot to me if you came, I'll buy you a beer, a big one.*

It turned out she preferred coffee. We sat at the same table where I bumped into Hase the first time. His hair was long now, it suited him. He tucked it behind his ears whenever it fell down in front of his eyes, it made his face seem narrower. His eyes were a very bright blue. I hadn't noticed they were that blue before. It might have been because he'd got such a tan. It had been sunny every day for three weeks.

'You've got a tan, Hase,' I said.

'That'll be the sunbeds,' he said with a laugh, and she laughed too. It was a giggly laugh and I joined in.

'Ha, ha,' I said.

'No, actually I've been sitting in the courtyard reading a lot lately,' he said.

'It's lovely that courtyard,' I said.

'Yes, it is,' he said. 'Then last Saturday I was at Nyhavn all afternoon with an old friend of mine.'

'Your trumpeter friend?' I said.

'Do you play the trumpet, Hase?' she said.

'He couldn't if he tried,' I said with a laugh, and Hase laughed too, he shook his head, his hair fell out from behind his ears again.

We were going to go through the fugue poem. Hase had made copies for us and we sat reading it to ourselves. She sipped her coffee while she read. Then she needed to go to the bathroom. She smiled and got up. She took her bag with her.

'How come you don't like her?' said Hase.

'I do like her.'

'I think she's very perceptive.'

'She's a bit smarmy. With that hair, and everything.'

'It's just her style.'

'I wouldn't call it that,' I said, and he sucked his cheeks in and leaned back against his trench coat. I tried to concentrate on the poem, I put a couple of exclamation marks in the margin with my marker pen and underlined something else. She came back from the bathroom. She'd put lipstick on, a dark red. She giggled as she sat down again.

'Well,' she said. 'I'm not a poet myself.'

'No,' said Hase.

'What are you, then?' I said.

'I write prose.'

'Short prose,' said Hase.

'Other things as well,' she said.

'You mean short stories?' I said.

'No, short prose. And other things as well,' she said. 'But I really think this poem has a lot going for it. You've worked hard on the cadence. You should cut down on the adjectives, though.'

'Yes, the pale hand is probably overdoing it a bit,' said Hase.

'That's one example,' she said. 'Try seeing what happens if you use hand on its own. It might be enough. Usually you can make do with a lot less.'

'There's got to be some flesh, though, surely?' I said.

'Not if there's no need,' she said. 'That's how I work, anyway. I'm always asking myself why does this have to be there, why does that have to be there? And if I can't find a reason, it goes.'

'Oh, right,' I said. Hase nodded.

'I suppose that's the best advice I can give. Lots of things sound good, and anything can go into a text. Anything you like. But there has to be a reason. Anyone can have a funny little man in a hat wander in.'

'Or a budding writer. Or a woman on a moped,' I said. Hase looked at me.

'Exactly,' she said.

'I'm not sure I agree with you on that,' I said. 'Sometimes things happen.'

'Yes,' she said. 'But that's only in reality. And here we're talking about fiction.'

She was meeting someone on Havnegade at four o'clock, so it was a brief appraisal. We both got up and shook her hand, Hase went to the counter and got two large beers. I looked out onto Axeltorv. There were flowers in the hanging baskets now, they looked like the ones in Haslev. People sat around chatting or stood looking at the water sculpture. Hase put a glass down in front of me. It was filled to the brim.

'Just the two of us now.'

'Yes.'

'Now we can have a beer and catch up.'

'Yes,' I said and took a big sip. Now that we were on our own again I felt relieved and more at ease.

'This ought to end at the Tivoli Gardens,' I said, putting down the glass, and he smiled at me over the rim of his own.

'It's all in your hands,' he said.

42.

I wrote too much about that doorway. Where I stood with a picnic basket full of kitchen utensils. Where I looked out at Knud. There he was, walking down the middle of the road to the station with my tartan suitcase. I followed on behind him, the air was warm and mild.

He put the suitcase down on the platform, then turned and raised his hand in a wave. I raised mine too.

'Thanks for your help. Best of luck,' I shouted.

'Write,' he shouted back, running sideways towards the office, a customer was waiting inside. He kept waving, and then he disappeared through the door.

There was a rumble in the distance. The lilacs were in bloom. This should be written in the present tense. I didn't write.